THE SLEIGH ON SEVENTEENTH STREET

Three Rivers Ranch Romance, Book 14

LIZ ISAACSON

Copyright © 2018 by Elana Johnson, writing as Liz Isaacson

All rights reserved.

No part of this book may be reproduced in any form or by any electronic or mechanical means, including information storage and retrieval systems, without written permission from the author, except for the use of brief quotations in a book review.

ISBN-13: 978-1728888811

SCRIPTURE

"Blessed are the peacemakers: for they shall be called the children of God."

— MATTHEW 5:9

CHAPTER ONE

Dylan Walker parked his truck and peered through the windshield at the mobile trailer that had been set up. Beyond that sat the Texas wilderness with trees, wild grasses, and beautiful flowers. A sour sensation coated his stomach. He couldn't believe the City Council had approved this development. Hundred-year-old trees would be lost. More of Three Rivers to enjoy, sure, but less of nature. And that didn't sit right in Dylan's gut.

Once he got out of the truck and made it a few steps, the highway that led out to Three Rivers Ranch glistened in the morning light. It had rained earlier, and the scent of dust and water mingled in the air.

Dylan took a deep breath and said a silent prayer. *Please let us get this bid.* He'd been working on the electrician bid for this new housing development for a solid month. The city desperately needed the contract, and he wanted to be the one to bring it to them.

With the project taking over two years, with four stages as new homes, twin homes, and condos went in, Dylan wanted to be in every residence, wiring every light and every surround sound system.

He shouldn't care so much. He'd get paid no matter what. But he and his boss had developed a plan to increase the public perception of the Three Rivers Electric Company, and if they won this bid, it would go a long way in proving to the citizens that the Electric Company was dedicated to providing excellent electrical customer service to all residents.

Dylan squared his shoulders, climbed the steps to the door, and entered the trailer. How the door had kept so much chaos concealed was a mystery. Dylan's head swiveled left and right as he took in the mob before him.

He recognized a dark-haired man, who'd come from Amarillo to bid on the electrical work for the build. Dylan had seen him—and lost a bid to him—at an office building last year. His mood darkened when he caught sight of yet another competitor, this one approaching him.

"Hiya, Dylan," the man said. Darrel maybe? Dallin?

"Hey," Dylan said, going with a more masculine greeting and bypassing the man's name completely. It wasn't like they were friends.

"You got your bid?" Darrel-or-Dallin nodded toward the folder Dylan held.

He clutched it tighter, a blip of annoyance coasting through him. "Yeah." Everyone here had a bid. Saddleback Homes had announced six weeks ago that they'd be taking bids for one day only. Eight hours. They'd look at all of them by the following day, when all the contractors, plumbers, electricians, and tradesmen had to be present in order to accept the bid.

Dylan had never seen anything like their process. He supposed it would make things go faster, and he'd cleared his schedule for tomorrow, his hopes high.

He'd arrived at the build site fifteen minutes early, thinking he might be the only one in the trailer for a few minutes, hoping to have a chance to speak with the manager of the project for a moment.

That wasn't going to happen. Dylan moved away from the door when someone opened it behind him. Thankfully, the other electrician got lost in the crowd. Dylan glanced around, his claustrophobic tendencies rearing themselves against the back of his throat. His pulse accelerated, and the sea of people and noise and activity before him started to blend into one giant wall of color.

He made a beeline for the door, glad for the cooler air outside of that room. It couldn't be bigger than a railcar, yet it held at least two dozen people. Dylan leaned against the railing and sucked in lungful after lungful of oxygen.

"Dylan Walker," a woman said, and he blinked.

His blurred vision took several moments to refocus, and when it did, he soaked in the form of Camila Cruz standing on the second step from the top. Golden-brown eyes he could swim in if she'd let him. Waves of nearly black, wavy hair. Yards of dark skin. *Fiery Latina temper*, he reminded himself as she did not look pleased to see him, which somehow made her more attractive.

"Cami." Dylan had entertained thoughts of dating Camila

a few years ago, but she had one massive chip on her shoulder during a project they'd completed together. She was headstrong, and stubborn, and bossy. Beautiful, absolutely. And Dylan didn't mind a strong, take-charge kind of woman. But Camila put off a vibe that said she definitely wasn't interested in him, so he'd kept his thoughts to himself.

Cami worked for the only plumber in town, a mom and pop joint that relied on the residents of Three Rivers to stay afloat. A winning bid for a project this size would allow Abraham and Dana Rogers to retire. Maybe that was why Cami looked like she'd swallowed poison and was about to throw up.

"Why are you out here?" she asked.

"Lots of people in there," he said, adding a shrug to the sentence so it would seem more casual. "I figure I have eight hours to put in my bid. I don't need to stand in line or practice my pitch."

She nodded and finished climbing the steps. Though she wore a gray T-shirt and jeans, Dylan still noticed her curves as she passed him and opened the door. The noise coming from inside nearly convinced him to leave and come back later, but he couldn't go back to the office without turning in the bid. His boss would fillet him with a single look.

So he followed Cami into the trailer, noticing how rigid she stood. "Told ya," he said.

"There are at least four other plumbers here," she said, her gaze swinging around the way his had.

"It's a big project."

"As if I didn't know." She rolled her eyes and hipped her way through the crowd to the far end of the trailer, where a table had been set up. Dylan watched her, almost intoxicated by the leftover whiff of perfume she'd left behind and the capable way she found what she was looking for.

He finally tore his gaze from her when she glanced over her shoulder to where he stood, as if she could somehow feel him watching her. He took a deep breath and looked around the trailer. He realized that hardly anyone held a folder the way he did. They were mingling and talking and looking at huge posters that had been put on the walls, detailing the phases of the build.

He moved through the press of bodies until he got to the end of the trailer too. A single man stood behind the table, which bore trays labeled *Plumbing, Electricity, Floors, Painting, General Contractors*, and several more titles.

He put his folder in the appropriate tray, ready to leave. These other men—and Cami—might not have anything to do for the rest of the day, but Dylan did. He turned to go, nearly mowing Cami to the ground in the process. Why was she standing so close?

"Sorry," he mumbled, sidestepping her and getting out of that trailer.

That evening found him at home, without Boone's pets to take care of. Without anything to eat, as his mom hardly cooked at all anymore. But when she did, Dylan ate like a king for days. Boone too. And Boone's dogs.

Dylan could put together scrambled eggs and toast, so he did that. He sometimes went over to his best friend's house to watch a baseball game, but there wasn't a game he cared about tonight. And now that Boone and Nicole were dating, Dylan wasn't always welcome in the evenings.

With summer in full swing and the holidays on the horizon, Dylan only had loneliness to look forward to. He'd attend Labor Day barbeques, Halloween parties, and Thanksgiving dinner at his parent's house on the other side of town with all three of his sisters, their husbands, and all of their kids.

Two of them still lived here in Three Rivers, and the other lived in Amarillo, only a half an hour away. Every Sunday was like Thanksgiving, and the thought of attending another family get-together by himself—even if he did love playing with his nieces and nephews—made him grumpy.

The TV blared in front of him, but he wasn't paying attention to it. He mentally ran through the female prospects in his life. He needed someone to take to the next family event, if only so he wouldn't have to go alone.

He'd dated several women in town, and since he'd grown up right here in Three Rivers, some girls were off the table. He may have dated them in high school, or they knew too much about him, or he them.

Round and round he went, and the only name he could come up with was Camila.

"Don't be ridiculous," he muttered to himself as he took his empty plate into the kitchen. He left it in the sink, along with the rest of his dishes from that week. He'd get to them on Sunday morning, the way he always did.

"Cami will chew you up and spit you out." Dylan stood in his kitchen, the rest of the house silent, empty, sad. Maybe he needed someone to challenge him. Maybe—he scoffed and returned to the couch. He wanted the Saddleback project, and he wanted someone to talk to at night. Didn't mean that person was Camila Cruz, and he found himself hoping that she didn't win the plumbing bid.

Guilt threaded through him, but he managed to calm it enough to fall asleep. His dreams featured a honey-eyed woman, whose waves of dark hair flew behind her as she walked toward him. She wore a plumbing tool belt, and she was still the most beautiful thing Dream-Dylan had ever seen.

CHAPTER TWO

Camila wiped her hand across her forehead, her fingers coming away slick with sweat. "You need a new faucet," she said as she straightened. The housewife who met her eyes had worry in hers.

"How much will that be?"

"You can go get one yourself, and I can install it for...." Camila pulled out her phone, glad this house had air conditioning blowing from the overhead vent. Some of the older homes in Three Rivers didn't, which made working on leaks under kitchen sinks nearly unbearable.

She tapped a few times on her phone, activating the price list from Rogers Plumbing. "One-thirty," Cami said. "If you want me to grab the standard faucet from our place, it'll be an inflated price." She looked up into the woman's face. "It's cheaper to go to the hardware store and get the faucet you want and just have me install it."

The other woman nodded. "I'll do that."

"Great." Cami put a smile on her face. "Let me know when you have it, and I'll swing by and get it installed."

"How long does that take?"

"Half an hour. I can squeeze you in." She pocketed her phone and picked up the work order board she'd brought inside with her. A little girl no older than five came down the stairs and to her mother's side.

Cami gave them both the warmest smile she could muster and headed for the front door. The bid announcements were starting in an hour, and she needed to grab something to eat before she went back up to the build site on the northeast side of town.

Her stomach turned over at the thought of putting anything in her mouth. Okay, so maybe eating before the bid winners were announced was a poor idea. She skipped the stop at her house for the peanut butter sandwich she'd made that morning and went back to the plumbing storefront on Main Street. Dana would be there, as she ran the storefront for anyone who came in and took all the service calls.

Her husband, Abraham, was getting close to retirement and he didn't usually come into the shop until later in the day. His arthritis had been flaring up in this mid-autumn Texas heat too, and Cami reminded herself to get a batch of tamales down to him that evening.

"Hey," she said, putting the work order clipboard on Dana's desk. The older woman looked up and smiled, her dark hair salted with gray. "The Fletchers are going to get a faucet and call when they're ready to have me come install it. I'm headed up to the Saddleback build site to see if we won the bid."

Dana slid the work orders toward her and smiled. "How long will you be up there?"

"I honestly don't know," Cami said, her nerves firing again. She'd seen her ex-boyfriend in the trailer the previous day, and she'd tried hiding behind Dylan's broad shoulders so Wade wouldn't see her. And she'd nearly been trampled by Dylan after he tossed his bid in the tray and turned to go.

"I've never seen a builder do bids like this before," Cami said, hoping Wade would send someone else from his plumbing shop in Amarillo. *Stop thinking about Wade*, she commanded herself. The man didn't deserve more than a moment of her attention, and she'd given him a lot more than that over the years.

"Hopefully not too long," Cami said. "I mean, they're just announcing who won. I don't expect there will be a debate." She'd never been able to adjust her bid once a contractor was selected, and she didn't see why Saddleback would do that in this situation.

What she did see was that the Rogers's needed this bid to stay open. Sure, installing new toilets and fixing pipes had kept them afloat for the better part of three decades. Their big repairs like fixing sewer pipes and re-plumbing the older homes sustained them through the leaner months.

But with all the new building happening in Three Rivers, they needed to be doing all the plumbs in those construction sites, or they'd become obsolete.

"I'll see you later," she said, turning to go before she allowed her desperation to infect her expression.

"Let me know how it goes," Dana called after her.

Cami arrived at the site, seemingly the last one there, just like yesterday. Today, the builders had set up two large tent shades, with rows of white folding chairs underneath. She groaned as she stepped from her air-conditioned work van. She slammed the door, and the resulting rattle reminded her that she needed to be more careful with Penny. Penny-the-Plumbing-Van had been with her since she'd started with Rogers Plumbing, nearly four years ago. Penny was getting older, was an excellent friend, and did the bulk of the heavy lifting when it came to carrying the equipment Cami needed.

She affectionately patted the hood as she rounded the van and scanned the shady areas for a seat—and Wade's dark hair. He sat on the left side, near the front, and she ducked toward the back, hoping he hadn't seen her yesterday. She'd followed Dylan right back out of the trailer and taken refuge in Penny until she'd calmed enough to go to her next job.

At that moment, she caught sight of Dylan Walker's shock of blond hair. Her feet paused. He had an empty seat next to him. He was the only person she knew here, and though she didn't particularly like him—in fact, almost everything about the man irritated her—her feet took her in his direction, because he was sitting on the far right, near the back. As far from Wade as Cami could get.

"Can I sit here?" she asked.

Dylan glanced up at her, and his blue-green eyes punched her right in the chest. His beautiful eyes didn't irritate her, and a little flutter started in her stomach.

"Sure." He grinned and shifted slightly on his seat as if he needed to make room for her to sit in his lap.

Cami pulled her phone from her back pocket and sat. So he had nice eyes—and a killer smile. Didn't mean she was interested in him. She'd heard enough stories from enough women to know that Dylan wasn't looking for a serious relationship.

Neither are you, Cami told herself. Her last attempt at serious had ended disastrously, with her moving from Amarillo to Three Rivers and knocking on the Rogers's door the next morning, begging for a job.

She cleared her throat and focused on the podium that had been set up at the front.

"Nervous?" Dylan asked.

She let out a very nervous chuckle. "Yes." She slid a look in his direction, long enough to catch the set line of his mouth but not long enough to truly admire his handsome features. "You?"

"Totally." He wiped his palms down his thighs. "And they put us outside to melt in the heat. Like we're not already sweating enough." His disgruntled words made her smile.

"I've been sweating since six this morning," she said.

"Oh yeah?" He leaned slightly toward her. "Why's that?"

"I do kickboxing in the mornings," she said, facing him fully and arching her right eyebrow.

A smile with the wattage of the sun beamed across his face. "Sounds…fierce."

"And then I've been in and out of cupboards all morning." Her stomach growled, but she ignored it.

"And you skipped lunch," he said with a chuckle. "Me too." He faced the front again, and Cami took comfort in the fact that he was as worried about winning the bid as she was.

"If you win, we should celebrate," he said, his voice much quieter than before.

She jerked away from him and looked at him. He didn't look at her but kept his focus up front. The only indication that he was talking to her came in the slight lean toward her chair.

Cami settled back into her seat properly. "What does that mean?"

"Dinner," he said. "Me and you."

She wanted to eat everything she could get her hands on after this bid, whether she won or not. Her compulsive need to eat—whether she was happy or sad, had lots of money or none, had had a good day or a bad one—was why she got up at five o'clock in the morning and worked out with a weight bag and a personal trainer.

Cami knew there were better ways to deal with her emotions, but she hadn't quite found one that worked for her yet.

"I'm not going to dinner with you," she hissed as a suit from Saddleback Homes stood and started making his way toward the podium.

"Even if I win the bid?" he asked.

"*Especially* if you win the bid," she said. She couldn't imagine how arrogant he'd be then. He'd probably jump up and shout if the city won the electric bid.

He chuckled like her rejection didn't even faze him, like his heart was made of steel and her words had bounced right off. No wonder he'd had four girlfriends in six months.

You don't know if that's true, she told herself as she folded her arms and crossed her legs. Trying to clench all her emotions inside, she took a deep breath, but that only filled her nose with the woodsy, wild scent of Dylan's cologne.

"Is that smell your cologne or a toxic spill?" she whispered.

Dylan didn't have time to answer before the suited man adjusted the microphone for his height and said, "Welcome to the Saddleback Homes Rivers Merge Development." He had a round, smooth voice that should've soothed Cami but didn't. "My name is Thomas Martin, and I'm the lead architect on this build." He smiled but it didn't carry any warmth.

Someone approached and handed him an envelope. "And now I have the winning bidders in my hand."

The crowd shifted and murmurs swam from the front to the back. Beside her, Dylan straightened, his gaze singular on that envelope.

Thomas ripped it open and extracted several sheets of paper. Cami released the breath she'd been holding. They'd start with the bigger companies first, like cement and brick masons, the landscapers, and then move to the smaller things inside: the electricians, the plumbers, the painters, the tile masters.

Still, she paid rapt attention to the companies and point-of-contact names as Thomas read them. If she won the bid for Rogers Plumbing, she'd be working with all of these... men. It hit her square in the face that every person under the tent was a man, except for her.

Her anxiety flipped up, and she worked to calm it. She'd spent her entire career working for men and with men. This would be no different. It would simply be two years of working with the *same* men as they built the one-hundred-ten unit development.

Cami tried to swallow, but her throat wasn't cooperating.

She needed this to keep the Rogers's relevant, keep her job in Three Rivers secure. *They* needed it so they could retire. They had three daughters, all married and living in the Hill Country. Cami wasn't sure if one of them would return to Three Rivers and take over the family business, but it was on her list of things to discuss with the Rogers's. They just needed to get through this bid first.

"Electric work," Thomas said, and Dylan's head jerked up from the notebook where he'd been taking notes. "Will be done by Three Rivers Electric Company." Thomas scanned the crowd until his eyes landed on Dylan.

Without thinking, Cami reached over and squeezed his knee. "Congratulations, Dylan."

He wore a smile just as wide as the one previously, but it carried only joy and no heat. That fact registered in her brain, but she didn't know what to make of it. Was he truly interested in her? Could they really go to dinner and have a good time?

"Plumbing work," Thomas said, and Cami almost bolted. She couldn't bear to hear another plumber—someone from outside Three Rivers—named, and she suddenly had no confidence that her bid had been good enough.

"Indoor and outdoor plumbing, for the entire community, will be done by Rogers Plumbing," Thomas said, the last two words reverberating around the tent.

Cami's heart stopped. Just full-on stopped pumping.

Thomas met her eyes, and gave a small nod of acknowledgement, and her pulse raced forward again.

"Congrats, Cami," Dylan said, not an ounce of sarcasm in his voice. He beamed at her. "You sure we can't go to dinner?"

Maybe my toxic spill cologne has driven away your appetite. I could shower before we go."

Her mind raced as fast as her heart was galloping. Something sparked between her and Dylan in that moment. That very moment when he had those deep, ocean-colored eyes trained right on her, and a gentle yet sure smile on his face, and that *so-not-a-toxic-spill* cologne wafting between them.

Oh, yes, something very hot sparked between them, reminding Cami that water and electricity didn't mix.

But she couldn't help the smile pulling against the corners of her mouth. She felt positively giddy when she said, "Yeah, let's go to dinner."

CHAPTER THREE

Dylan waited with the other winning bidders in the air-conditioned trailer. A container of iced sweet tea sat on the back table, and everyone had helped themselves to some and now stood in little clumps, talking.

He stuck close to Cami for a reason he couldn't name. "This is interesting tea," she said, staring down into her cup.

"It has a lot of orange in it," he agreed. He was a sweet tea purist—lemon and honey only for him.

"And mint." Cami made a face and set her cup on the table behind them.

Saddleback had chosen to stay with all local Three Rivers companies for this build, and as Thomas entered the trailer, Dylan once again thought he looked familiar.

Thomas shook hands with the people nearest him, the brick mason who currently had two employees—his two sons. How they would handle the brickwork for the entire community was beyond Dylan. But he was thrilled they'd won the bid. Their family dynasty in the business would be able to continue because of it.

"Welcome," Thomas finally said. "I trust you are all thrilled to be working with us on this new development."

Acknowledgements spread through the crowd. "We're excited to be working with so many local tradesmen, so much Three Rivers talent." He sent his chilled smile throughout the room. "My family lived here when I was younger, and the sense of community has stuck with me though they moved when I was only twelve."

Thomas Martin, Dylan thought. His brain whirred. "Thomas Martin," he whispered. He seemed so familiar, and yet Dylan couldn't locate a memory with him in it.

"You know him?" Cami inched closer to him. So close Dylan's next breath was filled with the scent of pineapple and something crisp. Eucalyptus? Peppermint?

"He grew up here until he was twelve," Dylan said, tilting his head toward Thomas. "You think he's that much older than me?"

She cocked her head and studied Thomas as he continued to speak. "He's probably between thirty-five and forty."

"I'm thirty-four," Dylan said.

"Really?"

"Really." Dylan focused back on Thomas, but still his memory failed him. An architect who used to live in Three Rivers didn't matter. He'd won the bid for the city and gotten a date with Cami. Today couldn't get any better.

He collected the contracts he needed to get signed, and he stepped back into the Texas heat with Cami right in front of him. "Hey, so maybe I can get your number," he said as she started down the steps.

She slipped, stumbled forward, and skidded down several steps before coming to a stop.

"Whoa, hey, you okay?" He hurried down in front of her and looked up to find surprise and horror on her face. She hadn't fallen, but she wasn't moving either. A blush crept into her cheeks, making her already bronze skin a delightful shade of brick red.

Dylan lifted his phone toward her. "So I can call you and let you know what time. I have to go back to the office, and I don't know how long I'll be." He swallowed, suddenly wishing he had his sweet tea back, though he hadn't really liked the addition of the orange. At least his voice was working.

When she just stared at his phone like it was a poisonous snake, he added, "I'm sure you have to get back to the Rogers's."

That launched her into motion. She ignored his phone and extended hers instead. "You can put your number in mine."

He didn't see what difference it made, so he took her phone and put in his number. "Great." He flashed her a smile he hoped would make her soften, just the tiniest bit. "See you tonight."

Dylan walked away, an extra bounce in his step that hadn't been there for months. Maybe years.

∼

Dylan whistled as he parked his truck and strode into the Electric Company. Asher had texted him three times, and Dylan hadn't answered. He burst into the man's office now and lifted the bulky contract above his head.

"Is that what I think it is?" Asher stood so fast, his chair flailed wildly into the wall.

"We won the bid." Dylan laughed, the heaviness he'd been dragging around with him for the past month finally lifting.

"We won the bid." Asher took the contract from Dylan and folded back the front cover. He muttered as he read the verbiage, saying coherent things like, "due by five o'clock PM by October fifth…duration of twenty-five months from the date of signing…all interior and exterior electrical needs of the Complex, including special wiring for hot tub pads and the community spa."

He glanced up, his dark eyes filled with happiness. "Great work, Dylan. Let's get this signed and back over to them."

Dylan eyed the inch-thick stack of papers and glanced at the clock on the wall behind Asher's desk.

Already three-thirty. He'd be lucky if he made it home before six, and then he had to shower….

He reached for his phone to reschedule with Cami, only to remember that she wouldn't give him her number. A smile curved his lips. He liked her fire, her strength, the fact that she went kick-boxing every morning.

"All right," Asher said, drawing Dylan away from the beginning of his fantasies. "There's a pen." He tossed a blue pen toward him.

"I'm signing?" Dylan just stared at his boss.

"I'm making you the point man on this," Asher said. "I don't have time to handle phone calls and meetings for a two-year project. You're the lead contact. You sign." Asher softened the slightest bit. "And I'm not going to be here forever. Someone has to know how every aspect of how this utility runs."

"And you think I'm—I mean, of course I can do that." But of course Dylan had never thought about being over the Electric Company. Sure, he'd worked there for sixteen years —straight out of high school. Did a four-year on-the-job apprenticeship with Asher and had been serving the citizens of Three Rivers ever since, horseback riding in the evenings and on the weekends, and he'd also recently started volunteering out at Courage Reins, with their veteran program on Tuesdays and Thursdays.

Asher sat down, a parental look on his face. "You've been here the longest out of anyone, besides me," he said. "I only have a few years left before Martha makes me retire and take her across the country in an RV. I need to be able to leave everything we've built in good hands."

Dylan sat down, his excitement peaking. "I have good hands."

Asher chuckled. "Well, let's get them signing this paperwork."

It was six-fifteen when Dylan left the office, a cramp in his right hand that wouldn't go away. Cami hadn't called or texted, and he wondered if she would. When he reached the apartment building where he lived, he wasted no time stepping into the shower. That way, on the off-chance that she did call, he'd be ready. And if she didn't, he could go grab something and eat it in the park.

His phone buzzed as he pulled on a clean pair of jeans. It wasn't a number he had in his phone, but the message clearly indicated it was from Cami. His heart lifted toward the ceiling.

Barely left work, she said. *I have a few questions before I agree to meet you somewhere for dinner.*

His heart crashed back to the floor. She wanted to *meet* him for dinner? Did women even consider meeting someone a date? Why was he even thinking about dating?

He shook his head and thumbed out, *Happy to answer anything.* While she typed, he pulled on a blue and white striped polo and dug through his drawer for a pair of socks.

His phone sounded his notification for a text—the sound of a baseball bat cracking a home run—and he swiped it off the dresser to read *Fact or false: You've been out with three women in the past four months.*

Dylan simply stared at the words. The letters rearranged themselves until all Dylan could see was *player*.

She thought he was a player!

Fury combined with frustration in his gut, rising up to his throat as he practically slammed his fingers on the letters to spell out *false*.

He really wanted to ask her where she'd gotten that misinformation too, but he wanted to be face-to-face with her when he did. Then he could watch her body language, her eyes, really see how she felt. Sometimes texting wasn't the best form of communication for serious topics.

Dylan knew. The reason he hadn't been out with anyone in a lot longer than four months, thank you very much, was because his last relationship with Althea, a third grade teacher at the elementary school, had ended over a text. As if the four months they'd shared together didn't require a real, grown-up conversation.

Fact or false: You only like blondes.

Clearly false, he sent, already tired of this game.

Fact or false: You kissed Shania Titan behind the bleachers in high school.

High school? Dylan felt like he'd been transported back almost two decades, and he looked up to the ceiling as if God Himself would be there to lend Dylan some patience.

And that one was true, and Dylan had never denied it. Never even wanted to. How did she know about Shania anyway? Camila had only been in Three Rivers for a few years. He still remembered the first time he'd met her, spitting fire and Spanish at him like he'd run over her cat.

He hadn't, of course. But he had arrived at the diner before her and had just uttered, "Looks like some water got in there and shorted things out."

She'd taken it as a personal attack and said, "Hey, it's not my fault that pinball machine shorted out."

Dylan could still remember the fire in her golden eyes, the way she filled out the tank top with ROGERS PLUMBING across the chest. So maybe he'd checked her out that first time they'd met. Could she blame him? She *kick-boxed* every morning, and she had legs, arms, and curves to prove it.

That one's true, he texted. *I'd love to tell you all about it over pizza.*

I'm a vegetarian.

Dylan exhaled as he sat on the edge of his unmade bed. Of course she was. He loved meat, so she wouldn't eat it. He wondered for a brief moment if trying to start something with Cami was harder than it should be.

Then he remembered the spark that had passed between them after he'd joked about his cologne. He got up and splashed some of the "toxic spill" on his neck.

Where do you want to go? he asked her.

They make a great veggie lovers pizza at this place in Amarillo.

Amarillo? Dylan glanced at the clock, not that he had anything else to do or anywhere to be before nine tomorrow morning. And it was only seven-fifteen.

Want me to come pick you up and drive? he messaged.

That would be great. I only have Penny.

Penny? Dylan stepped into the bathroom to comb his hair and brush his teeth.

My plumbing van.

Dylan chuckled as he grabbed his keys and wallet from the kitchen counter and headed out to his truck.

I just need your address.

She sent it, and Dylan couldn't help the grin that graced his face as he drove the few blocks from his apartment to her house. She lived in the older section of town, in a cute little cottage she clearly kept up in her after-work hours.

Large trees guarded the property along the road, creating

a lot of shade in the evenings. Her grass had seen better days, but it was the tail end of summer, and all the lawns in Three Rivers looked like hers. At least the bark in her flowerbeds looked fresh.

He climbed the few steps to her small porch and wiped his hands down his thighs. He knocked, unsure of what to expect when she opened the door.

But it was not a brunette bombshell wearing a blood red tank top that seemed welded to her skin. And her skin.... Dylan wanted to trail his fingers over it to see if it was as silky soft as it looked. A light cocoa color, her skin was only complimented by the red tank. She wore a tight pair of black jeans, with bright red heels on her feet.

Her toenails were not painted, and she hadn't made up her face much more than usual. Definitely some darker mascara on her eyes, and her lips seemed to be glossed with raspberries. Dylan swallowed, his mouth watering for a taste of her. She looked nothing like a plumber and everything like the kind of woman Dylan wanted. And wanted very badly.

"Wow," he finally said after he'd drunk her in several times. "Don't you clean up nice?"

She smiled, revealing straight white teeth, and nudged him backward as he started to inch toward her. "So do you."

His chest burned where she'd touched him, even through the cloth of his shirt. She joined him on the porch, which shrank instantly. He took her hand in his and cast her a look to judge her reaction.

Those delicious lips curved up, and she didn't try to pull her hand away. "So tell me about this veggie lovers pizza in

Amarillo," he said. "I might need to be convinced it's worth eating."

"After you tell me about Shania." She placed the toe of one heel on the running board of his truck. "Deal?"

He put his hands on her waist to brace her. He'd agree to whatever she wanted when she wasn't wearing men's work boots and baggy T-shirts with company logos on them. "Sure," he said. "It's not that exciting."

"Well, neither is veggie pizza." Camila gave him a sultry smile, pushed off, and slid into his truck like she'd made that exact move dozens of times before.

As Dylan hurried around to get behind the wheel, he hoped she would do exactly that dozens of times again.

CHAPTER FOUR

*D*ylan started talking when he turned onto the highway that led out of town. "I was sixteen when I kissed Shania. There wasn't a sixteen-year-old boy in the county that hadn't dreamt about it. A lot of us did it, too."

Cami just listened, the way Kacey had advised her to. Her best friend had grown up with Dylan, married a local boy right out of high school, and worked at the daycare now that she had two kids of her own.

"She was pretty, and when she invited me to go with her behind the bleachers, I didn't ask why. I knew why. Everyone knew why."

"Was she a good kisser?" Cami asked.

"My sixteen-year-old self thought so."

"And now?"

"Now?" Dylan glanced at Cami and back to the road. He drove with one hand draped over the steering wheel and the other with his elbow resting on the console that he'd pulled down between them.

He shrugged. "Now, I've kissed more women. Women, not girls."

"A lot, I've heard."

"Who are you talkin' to?" he asked with an easy smile. She wondered what it would take to ruffle him. "I haven't been out with anyone in eight months, and before that I dated a teacher for four months. Yes, we kissed. We were dating. But it's not like I have a new woman every other week."

Cami crossed her arms, her head bobbing a little bit like a toy. "Are we dating?"

"I picked you up, right? We're going to dinner. I'm counting this as a date." He spoke slowly, like he might spook her with the words.

And he did. She wasn't sure why, only that she hadn't dated anyone in a lot longer than eight months. She didn't want to tell him about Wade, though, so she pressed her lips together and got the disgusting taste of her lip-enhancing lip gloss. It made her lips fuller and the label called it Ripe Raspberry. Dylan had liked it. His gaze had lingered on her mouth for several long seconds.

Satisfaction sang through her that she could still get a man to look at her like she was a woman.

She frowned at herself. *Every* man she met looked at her like she was a woman. Some just wore more of a sneer when she was in her plumbing clothes. And she'd never gotten quite as dolled up for a date before.

But it was Dylan Walker, and there had been that

singeing spark.... So yes, Cami had pulled out the Ripe Raspberry and her sister-in-law's birthday present from last year. Suzie would be excited Cami had finally worn the crimson tank top.

"Are we done with fact or false?" he asked.

"Unless you want to ask me something," she said, instantly regretting the words.

He lifted one shoulder. "I'm good."

The tension inside her drained away, leaving only a calm silence between them.

"Brothers or sisters?" he asked.

"One brother. Oscar. He's married and works as a hospital administrator in Amarillo."

"Are you from Amarillo?"

"Yep. My parents still live there."

"Why'd you come to Three Rivers?"

His questions were harmless, just general things one would reveal about themselves on a first date. And that was exactly why Cami hadn't gone on any first dates in four years.

"I...needed a new job." Not a lie. She'd been forced to quit hers when things went south with Wade. His father owned the plumbing shop where Cami worked, and she'd have been fired if she hadn't quit.

Wade Wadsworth, or Double-Double as he wanted to be called, had a mean streak Cami didn't know about until she was in too deep. With her work and personal life all tangled up, it had taken her several long months before she'd been brave enough to confront Wade Wadsworth on his chauvinistic and inappropriate behavior toward her.

"How long have you been a plumber?" Dylan asked, skimming over why she needed a new job like he didn't care. Maybe he didn't.

"Ten years. Well," she said. "I did all my vocational training during my senior year and right out of high school. Then I started my apprenticeship with Wadsworth Plumbing in Amarillo. It was three years before I could take my exams, so I guess it's more like six years since I got the license."

"You don't seem that old to me," he said, cutting her a flirtatious look. "You can't be thirty yet."

"I will be on Christmas Eve," she said.

He nodded and the much larger town of Amarillo came into view. "So where am I going?" he asked.

"How familiar with Amarillo are you?"

"Very."

"So there's a little joint over on the east side of town."

"Tower of Pizza," they said together.

"I know it," Dylan said. "Never had the veggie lovers though."

"It's fantastic, with pesto instead of marinara sauce, artichoke hearts, Greek olives, mushrooms, and these caramelized onions...." She moaned. "It's *so* good."

"I've had their cheesesteak pizza. It's great."

"We can get half-and-half, if you want."

"Oh, I'll try the veggie lovers," he said. "I don't mind."

And Cami really didn't think he did.

The atmosphere inside the pizzeria was exactly as Cami remembered: vibrant, trendy, and filled with the scent of garlic and tomato sauce. She took a deep breath, a little bit of her soul reviving at being back here.

"I used to think I was so cool in high school when we came here." Cami smiled at Dylan and reached for his hand.

"It's a pretty cool place," Dylan said, glancing around.

"Two tonight?" A hostess grabbed two menus and led them through the dining room to a booth against the window. A romantic yellow light hung above the table, and the tinted windows made it seem darker and later than it actually was.

"We know what we want," Dylan said when the hostess handed him the menu.

"Great, your server will be right over."

"You really don't have to get the veggie lovers pizza," Cami said, a zing of worry shooting through her.

"I don't mind. I want to try it." Dylan leaned into the table, his turquoise eyes shining with the light. "So we won the bids. Can you believe it?"

Cami laughed, tipping her head back slightly. "I actually can't believe it. Dana couldn't believe it either." She leaned closer too. "She started crying." The moment between them sobered, and Cami dropped her gaze to the tabletop.

"What are they going to do?" Dylan asked.

"What do you mean?"

"Their daughters are all older than me," he said. "They've got to be close to retirement."

"I'm not sure," Cami said.

"Would they sell you the shop?"

"Who says I want the shop?" Cami couldn't help challenging him. But he spoke like he knew her, like he knew all the thoughts that had been tumbling through her head these past few months.

Dylan's eyebrows went up. "I guess you could start your own shop." He glanced up as the waiter arrived. They ordered sodas and the pizza they wanted, and the waiter whisked their menus away.

"Unless you're planning to leave Three Rivers." He reached across the table and took her hand in both of his. "Are you planning to leave Three Rivers?"

Cami met his eyes, suddenly wanting to be closer to him than the table between them allowed. "No," she said. "I like Three Rivers."

"So maybe you need to figure out what they're going to do with their shop." Dylan shrugged and leaned back, taking his warm hands with him.

The waiter arrived with their drinks, and he unwrapped his straw and downed half the glass before she even moved.

"Tell me about your family," Cami said, though she'd heard some things from her friends around town.

"I have three older sisters," he said. "All married. They all have kids. They all live nearby." The light in his eyes dimmed a little, and Cami wondered what that was about. She knew his oldest sister, Alecia, lived on the west side of town, near the orchards, and worked at the library.

She wasn't sure what else to ask, creating a lull in the conversation. Dylan hadn't looked away from her, and Cami knew why he'd drank so much of his soda. Her throat felt like it had been made of cotton and sand, so she took a long drink of her cola too.

"Can I ask you something?" he asked.

"Sure."

"You can say no," he said.

"Oh, boy." She flashed him a smile, but he didn't return it, which made her muscles tense again.

"So my sisters are...awesome," he said, and Cami knew he probably meant something else. "But they're all married, and they have great husbands, and I love my nieces and nephews. I do."

"All right." Cami didn't know where he was going with this.

"We get together every Sunday. All these big parties and barbecues and family meals." He gestured with his hands with each event his family did.

"You sound like you don't like it."

"It can be a lot," he said. "The next big event is a Halloween trick-or-treat-slash-barbecue my mother has been planning for two weeks."

Cami smiled at the edge of agony in his eyes. "You don't like a barbecue? How very un-Texan of you."

"I love barbecues," he said. "But I—I—would you come with me?"

The pizza arrived, saving Cami from answering right away. Halloween was a month away, and there was always loads of fruit and salads at barbecues. She'd be fine.

And surprisingly, she liked Dylan a lot more than she thought she did. Maybe the things she'd heard about him weren't all true. *Maybe none of them are true.*

The waiter left, and Dylan looked at her expectantly. "Are you going to take the first slice?" he asked, nudging the tray closer to her.

"I'll go to the barbecue with you," she said.

Dylan's smile was slow, and sexy, and sent a shiver through her stomach. "Thanks, Cami."

She reached for the pizza and took a slice, the scent of hot pesto meeting her nose and making her mouth water. Or maybe that was the man sitting across from her. She wasn't entirely sure.

She took a bite of the pizza, and her eyes rolled back in her head. "This is so good," she said even though her mouth was full.

He chuckled and took a slice too. "What was that? So good?" He took a bite and chewed slowly, thoughtfully. "It's not bad." He took another bite. "Would be better with some sausage though."

Thankfully, she'd just swallowed so that when her laughter burst from her mouth, it was food-free.

Surprise mingled with her happiness. She honestly hadn't expected to enjoy Dylan Walker's company as much as she was.

"Fact or false," she said. "You have pets."

"False," he said. "You?"

"Two cats."

"Of course."

"What does that mean?"

"If I had pets, they'd be dogs. I babysit Boone's dogs all the time."

"Boone, the vet?"

"Yeah."

"Fact or false," she said. "We'll find something we have in common." She wasn't sure they had anything in common—and she also wasn't sure she cared.

"Fact," he said, leaning closer, his eyes doing that intense burning right into her soul again. "I'll find something, Cami."

She appreciated his determination and ducked her head as heat rose into her face. He made her feel stronger than she normally did. Adored in a way she hadn't been in a long, long time—if ever. He made her feel feminine and beautiful and worthwhile.

"Besides, we already found something," he said. "This pizza." He reached over and took another slice with a tantalizing smile, and Cami felt like it was a little piece of her heart.

CHAPTER FIVE

"All right there, Henry," Dylan said, keeping a tight hold on the reins. "You ready to get up?" He beamed at the man in the wheelchair, and Henry, who was a good decade older than Dylan, smiled back.

"Oh, yeah, let me just hop on up." He kept his smile in place, and the shine in his dark eyes didn't dim. But Dylan wondered how he could joke about his condition. He'd lost both legs while he was serving in the Army overseas, and he never went anywhere without his dog, Chief.

Even now, Chief panted at his side, his eyes squinted as he gazed at Dylan like maybe he'd get a pat later. Dylan knew he wasn't supposed to pet the service dogs, but he also couldn't help himself.

It had been a while since he'd seen Leia and Vader, and he just liked pups so much. He should probably get one of his own. Take it running in the morning the way Boone did, or bring it out the ranch and let it run with the horses whenever he came.

The sun was going down fast, so Dylan didn't waste any time. After chuckling for a moment, he said, "You grab onto me real good this time." He'd almost dropped the Sergeant last time, and he wasn't going to do that again.

Henry unbuckled his lap belt and reached up, wrapping his powerful arms around Dylan's shoulders and back. Dylan lifted him with a grunt and the words, "Holy cow, man, you need to stop working out."

He got Henry into the saddle on Poppyseed's back, and the horse barely moved one hoof in the process. Dylan walked around and made sure Henry was belted onto the saddle, though he'd been coming to Courage Reins for over a year and was very good at horseback riding.

The last thing Dylan needed was an accident because he hadn't checked something. "All right." He handed the reins to Henry and asked, "What are you doing today?"

The man squeezed Poppyseed with his thighs, and Dylan kept his focus on the man's face instead of where his legs ended unnaturally.

"Pete said there was a new man coming today," Henry said. "Said I should partner up with him." He glanced over his shoulder, but there was no one else in the arena.

"Well, I'll get your chair out of the way," Dylan said, already reaching for it. "And go find out. You want to just circle here for a few minutes?"

"Sure." Henry clicked his tongue at Poppyseed, and the black and white horse started walking. Dylan watched Henry for a moment after he'd gone by him, a sense of something wonderful filling his chest.

This man hadn't given up. Hadn't quit just because life gave him something absolutely unfair and difficult. Dylan wanted to be like Henry, and as he moved the wheelchair out of the dirt and onto the cement, he thanked the Lord for all the good things—and bad things—in his life.

He found Pete at the doorway leading to the stables, another man with him. He walked with forearm crutches and didn't have a single hair on his head.

"Hey, there," Dylan said with a smile. "Pete, Henry's all saddled up."

"Good, great," Pete said. "See, Carl. And he doesn't have legs below the knee."

Carl looked like he'd swallowed poison and had just been told there was no antidote.

"I'll ride tandem, if you want," Dylan said, hoping it was a helpful suggestion.

"He's a bit...nervous around horses." Pete cut Dylan a glance, trying to communicate something. But Dylan didn't get the message.

"Oh, well, maybe you'd like...Sabrina to come do it?"

Carl looked at Dylan then. "Sabrina?"

"She's Cal's daughter," Pete said. "She's here this week, and she loves the horses."

"How old is she?" Carl asked.

"Oh, what now?" Pete asked with a sigh. "Ten, maybe?"

"She's real good with horses," Dylan said with an extra Texas twang in his voice. "They seem to listen to her before she even speaks."

Several long seconds passed before Carl said, "Well, if a child can do it...."

"I'll go get her," Dylan said. "Why don't you go pick your horse?" He grinned at Pete when he saw the man's bright green eyes sparkling. Maybe he'd gotten the message after all. "But if I were you, I'd go with Chocolate Kisses. That's Bri's favorite."

He walked away with a chuckle, glad when he heard the door leading to the stable close behind Pete and Carl.

He found Bri on the front porch of her cabin, slicing at a branch with a pocketknife. "Hey, Bri, baby."

"Dylan!" She launched herself off the steps, barely dropping the knife before he caught her.

They laughed together, and he said, "We got an Army guy who needs help with a horse. Can you go ask your daddy if you can come over to the stables?"

"Yeah, be right back." She skipped up the steps and came out only seconds later with her cowgirl hat on. "I just need to change my boots."

Katrina appeared in the doorway and said, "You'll miss dinner."

"I'll make sure she eats," Dylan said, though he had no idea how he would do that. Maybe Pete's wife would have something at the homestead near the pastures. "How are you, Trina?"

"Good, Dylan." She smiled at him, and he grinned back. "You?"

"Just fine."

"Heard you went out with someone the other night."

Dylan shook his head, though the smile remained on his

face. "How in the world would you know that? I didn't think you left this ranch."

"Very funny." She rolled her eyes good-naturedly. "But who was it?"

"The plumber, Cami Cruz."

"I don't know her."

"Yeah, well, I'm planning on cutting through the pipes in my kitchen sink just to see her again." He tipped his hat now that Sabrina had her boots on.

"So you like her," Trina folded her arms and a baby cried in the house.

"I sure do." Dylan took Sabrina's hand and they started to walk away. "Bye, Miss Trina," he called over his shoulder. "All right, Bri," he said as the gravel crunched under their boots. "This guy's name is Carl and he's a bit afraid of the horses."

"Why would anybody be afraid of horses?" she asked in a genuine need-to-know tone.

"Oh, baby, they're big. And they're tall. And he can't walk real good. You know?"

"I'll help him," she said, and Dylan knew she would. After all, the girl had a remarkable talent with horses and people alike, and there was nothing more Dylan liked than spending evenings at Courage Reins.

Unless, of course, he could spend the evening with Cami. But she hadn't called or texted after their date two nights ago, and he'd given her space.

But as he introduced Bri to Carl, he decided he'd definitely be calling Cami that night to see if they could get together again soon.

Only a few days later, Dylan showed up at the Rivers Merge development to put in the temporary electrical lines the builder needed to move forward with the project. Surprise darted through him to see Cami there, driving a yellow and black excavator.

His blood started pumping hard through his body at the sight of her dark ponytail swaying as she clawed at the ground.

Dang, she was skilled and beautiful—and she'd never answered his call from the other night. He'd thought they'd had a good time, too. Held hands a little. Chatted. Laughed. He hadn't found that thing they had in common, but he couldn't be expected to do so when he never saw her, could he?

"Hey," someone said, and Dylan startled his gaze away from Cami, realizing that he'd been staring for several long seconds.

"Hey," Dylan said turning to find Easton, a co-worker from the Electric Company. "Let's get this temporary line in." It took everything he had not to turn and watch the activity near the tree line.

"Looks like they're digging wells," Easton said. "I didn't realize this wouldn't be part of the town sewer system."

Dylan frowned, but he didn't say anything. He honestly had no idea what the plans were for this community. He'd been given his electrical specs, and he hadn't seen Cami since their dinner, so he had no idea what her plumbing plans looked like.

Wasn't his business anyway.

He and Easton got to work to bring electricity down from the power lines across the street. The green utility boxes that fed the homes that used to be the farthest ones north sat opposite him, and Dylan said, "Better get the road coned off."

Easton did that while Dylan got out his map for where the underground lines would be. It would take them almost two weeks to get the electrical boxes in place for this build, but he wasn't doing all of that today. Just getting the power from one side of the street to the other. He'd come in as they started building and add the power grid as they advanced through the construction phases.

Getting the power from there to here required busting through the asphalt road and digging down two feet. At least there were no sidewalks to be redone, and the public works department would send out the asphalt crew to patch this road until the construction was complete.

Easton had the green electrical box open and the breakers off before Dylan brought in the jackhammer to get the asphalt broken up. Thankfully, they only needed about a one-foot strip, and it only took a few minutes to get through the road.

Then they took to the trench with shovels. Dylan liked the hard work, the bend and dig and throw repeated motion of digging a trench for the wires. Sure, he went home tired at the end of every day, but he always felt good about what he'd accomplished.

"We'll need to see the plumbing specs," Easton said. "If they're doing well houses, those will require power."

Dylan lifted his head, the trench almost done. "That's true." He frowned and glanced back to where Cami had moved to a new spot of earth to abuse. The site hadn't been cleared or leveled yet, but Dylan knew it would be soon. In fact, by the time Dylan returned to Rivers Merge, it would look completely different. They'd leave him space to put his wires in the ground, but the plots would be leveled, staked, with foundations poured and plumbing started.

"I'll go ask her," he said, brushing his gloved hands together. Dylan left Easton to finish the trench and approached Cami in her powerful piece of equipment. He swallowed, trying to wet his throat before he spoke.

He waved to get her attention, and she nodded to acknowledge that she'd seen him. But she didn't cut the engine or stop working. In fact, she made Dylan wait an entire five minutes while she finished digging the well. Only then did she climb down from the excavator, wearing her ultra-tight yoga pants and a tank top the color of lemons.

Dylan licked his lips, his focus on hers, which shone with gloss under the mid-morning sun. "Are you doing wells in all the properties?" he asked.

"No, just five back here," she said, shielding her eyes with her hand as she looked up at him.

A smile curved his mouth. Her beauty made him ache with the need to kiss her. "Do you—they need power in the pump houses?"

"I'm sure they will. My job was to get the wells done today," she said, a definite edge in her voice.

He didn't need another repeated jukebox incident, so he took a step back when he wanted to lunge forward, wrap his arms around her, and bring her into his chest. "I'll check with the construction foreman. I didn't see powered pump houses in my specs."

He wanted to ask her about the unreturned phone call, but he didn't want to appear desperate.

Dylan turned and went back the way he'd come, taking a detour toward the construction trailer instead of returning to Easton, who had the two-by-fours out and was waist-deep in the earth to make sure they got seated correctly. It didn't rain or snow much here in Three Rivers, but Dylan and his crew always planned for the worst, especially heading into the winter months.

He'd climbed the steps and opened the door to the trailer before he realized Cami had come with him. His pulse *pa-*pumped an extra time, whether from nerves or her proximity, he wasn't sure.

"Gerald," Dylan said, keeping one eye on Cami as she flanked him. "Cami said there's five wells along the back of the build." He hooked his thumb over his shoulder but it was in the complete wrong direction. He dropped his hand to his side. "Are you planning to build powered pump houses for those?"

Gerald, a man close to fifty if Dylan had to guess, looked up from the desk against the wall. "Wells?"

"My specs had five wells along the back edge of the build," Cami said. "I just finished the third one."

Gerald shook his head as he rose. "That's an old spec. We're doing individual water for each unit. City sewer systems."

"An old spec?" Cami stepped forward, and all the alarms in Dylan's body and mind went off. Loudly.

"Why do I have an old spec?" she asked.

"I don't know." Gerald settled his weight onto the edge of his desk and folded his arms, completely unconcerned. Dylan wanted to yell at him to *run! Hide!* Because while he faced the back of Cami's head, he could *feel* the sizzling energy of her anger. It hung in the air like the scent of fried food at the town fair.

"I'll find out and get you the updated specs," Gerald said, sighing as he went back around his desk. He sat down and pulled a folder toward him, settling his glasses back into place. Conversation over.

"So I'm good," Dylan said loudly. "I'll just finish up that temporary power line, and—"

Cami spun around, her honeyed eyes anything but sweet. "What am I supposed to do with those holes?" She stared at him, but he knew she wasn't really asking him.

"Fill 'em in," Gerald said like it was just that easy. Like she hadn't spent almost half a day of her time digging them. Dylan would be mad too.

He tried to smile, but Cami rolled her eyes. "Fine." She stomped past him. "I'll fill them in."

Dylan followed her out, calling, "Cami."

She slowed but didn't turn around. He caught up to her easily. "Sorry about the outdated specs. Want me to help—?"

"I don't need your help, Dylan." Her words slapped him in the face, knocked the wind right out of his lungs, slowed his feet until they stopped. She kept going, marching with sure strides until she reached her excavator. She climbed in and started scooping dirt back into the hole she'd just made.

Fact or false: We'll find something we have in common.

Dylan watched her for a few moments past normal and then he returned to Easton and the job *he* was there to do. And it wasn't to help Cami with her outdated specs, or stare at her until it was obvious to everyone in town that he had a Texas-sized crush on the woman, or to try to find something they had in common.

He'd been about to ask her to lunch, but now he wondered if he should interact with her at all past what he had to in order to finish this project.

CHAPTER SIX

*C*ami sighed as she let the hot water run over her hair and back. Some might think it silly to shower before getting on a horse, but Cami couldn't possibly subject the poor creature to the smell of machinery and frustration.

So she showered and got in her two-seater sedan. Penny would never make it all the way out the Three Rivers Ranch, and while she hoped if they had a plumbing problem, they'd call her, she honestly doubted if her van would make it.

She pulled up to the stables on the north side of the street and got out, trying to exhale out the stress of her day.

Old specs.

How ridiculous. She doubted a man would've gotten old specs. At the very least, the manager would've apologized to a man. All she'd gotten was "Fill 'em in."

Which she'd done. It had taken another few hours, and she'd wasted so much time and money. The thought of it got her blood pressure up again, and she was supposed to be here to ride horses, release her cares to the atmosphere, and relax.

And she couldn't do that if she dwelled on work. She'd taken off early just to get over the catastrophe from that morning.

"And Dylan was there," she muttered. As if she needed another reason to look stupid in front of him. All the giggling and hand-holding from the other night made embarrassed heat shoot to her face every time she thought about it.

So much so that she hadn't been able to answer him when he'd called last night. And that just made her feel even worse when it came to him.

She sighed and Brynn Greene said, "There you are. You gonna come in and ride?"

Cami pushed one more breath out. "Yeah. Yes, I am." She didn't get on a horse nearly as often as she'd like to, but when she could get out here and breathe the fresh air, and brush down a horse, and remember that her life hadn't always been about trying to prove she was capable, she remembered how much she liked the small-town life.

"You want Valentine?" Brynn called on her way back into the building.

Cami followed her, saying, "Yes, please." She pushed through the door to find Brynn holding a little girl on her hip. "Oh, hey, there," she said, a bit awkwardly.

"Say hello, baby," Brynn said, but the girl said nothing. Brynn giggled and said, "Go on back, Cami. And if you want something to eat when you're done, just come down to the cabin."

"Thanks, Brynn." Cami very rarely stayed to eat with the Greene's, though Brynn asked her to every time she came.

She loved coming out here at the start of her weekend, though she worked just as many Saturdays as she took off. But Friday nights on horseback were perfect. It was still afternoon, but she figured a ride now would be just as wonderful as it would've been later.

She took slow steps down the aisle toward Valentine's stall, but the horse wasn't there. Cami turned to the other side of the aisle, and The Green Giant was gone too.

"Carole Anne," she said, a smile forming on her face. She started down the aisle and out the door, where sure enough, a blonde woman with the curliest hair on the planet stood in the pasture with both horses.

She was the quintessential cowgirl, with the short denim shorts and the cowgirl boots. Her hair was always piled in a curly, snaky mess on top of her head, and she wore sunglasses instead of a hat.

"Carole Anne," Cami called, her own cowgirl boots pinching a bit on her pinky toe on her right foot. She didn't wear the boots enough to have them completely broken in, even after several months of owning them.

Her friend always went by both names, and she turned toward Cami. "There you are."

Cami arrived and took the reins for Valentine. "Got off early?" she asked Carole Anne.

"Yeah, as always," she said. "There's too many of us at the grocer."

"You don't need to work anyway," Cami said.

"No, but it's good to get out of the house sometimes."

"You can come out here anytime you want." Cami swung into the saddle as she pushed back the jealousy. Carole Anne was literally the nicest person in all of Texas, and she just happened to have the perfect life.

At least on the outside.

Cami knew Carole Anne adored her husband, sure. And that he worked as a banker in town and she didn't need to work at all. They traded yard care tips while they sat on their front steps and chatted, so Cami also knew that Carole Anne had been told she could never have children, and that such a thing was as close to death for her as one could get.

So she was terribly lonely—by her own admission—and worked at the only grocery store in Three Rivers so she'd have some friends and adult interaction during the day.

And she rode with Cami most Friday evenings. She mounted her horse too, and they set off in the opposite direction of the sun.

"Congratulations on getting the bid," Carole Anne said after a few minutes.

Cami smiled. "Thanks." She didn't want to talk about the disaster that had happened today, choosing instead to go with the euphoria of winning the bid from earlier in the week.

"Should keep you plenty busy for a couple of years," Carole Anne said. "What with all the town work too."

"Yeah." Cami sighed. "I think Dana and Abraham will retire once it's done."

"You think they'll make it that long?"

"I don't know," Cami said.

"Will you buy their shop?"

Cami had thought a lot about doing exactly that. But she hadn't wanted to infringe on the Rogers'. They were good people, who'd spent a lifetime building their business. Who was she to come in and buy it?

"I'm going to talk to them," she said. "When the time is right." She flashed Carole Anne a smile, glad Valentine seemed to be in a lazy mood this afternoon. He plodded along with slow steps, and she barely held the reins in her fingers.

The silence out in the country soothed her, and they fell silent as their horses found some fresh grasses and started to nibble.

She thought about Dylan and if he'd ever come out and spend a lazy afternoon with the horses. He seemed like the kind of man who always had to be doing something, going somewhere, making things happen.

She'd watched him work for a few minutes that morning, and he certainly had muscles to set posts and dig trenches, and his work ethic clearly didn't need much improving. She found herself wondering what he did in his free time, and if he'd like to spend any of it with her.

"So," she said, making a quick decision. "I'm, well, I went out with a guy this week."

Carole Anne jerked her head toward Cami. "You did? Who?"

"Dylan Walker?" She looked at Carole Anne to judge her reaction. She'd grown up in the Three Rivers, and though Dylan was a few years older than her, she probably knew him or his family.

"Why, Dylan's good people," Carole Anne said. "His mom's one of the best cooks in the whole county."

Cami laughed like being a good cook was a requirement for being a good person. "I can barely make banana bread, but I still think I'm a decent person."

"You know what I mean."

"I actually have no idea what you mean." Cami grinned at her.

"The Walkers are a stable, church-going family," Carole Anne said. "They work hard, and they make cute babies."

Cami scoffed and shook her head. "Oh, wow. Well, we went on one date, so I don't think we're quite to talking about babies yet."

Carole Anne tsk'ed at her horse to get it to move again. "Come on, Greenie. No more grass." She waited for Cami to come up alongside her and then she added, "Is there going to be a second date?"

"I don't know." Cami watched the horizon now, hoping her face didn't show the heat creeping into her cheeks. "He called, and I didn't call him back."

"Why not? You don't think he's pretty much the cutest single man in town?"

"Is he?"

"Uh, yeah. Some of the other girls at the grocer have been plotting during their lunch hours for how they can get him to ask them out." Carole Anne giggled. "Apparently he hasn't gone out with anyone in a while, and they've been biding their time."

He hadn't had a problem asking her to dinner, and

another dose of warmth moved through her. "I should probably call him back, huh?"

"Uh, yeah. Unless you want Avery MacGuiver to get her hooks in him."

"Oh, no. Not Avery." Cami rolled her eyes. While Avery was one of the best singers in the church choir, that was about as far as her niceness went.

"See? You'd be saving him from an unsavory woman," Carole Anne said. "But not if you don't call him." She sang the last two words, and Cami couldn't help laughing with her.

"All right," she said. "I'll call him."

"When?"

Carole Anne knew her too well. "I don't know."

"Tonight."

"Really? Tonight?" It was Friday night. What would he think of her calling then? Would it show him she had nothing going on? What if he was out with someone else and didn't answer?

"I think tomorrow," she said.

"Nope," Carole Anne said. "I think you should call him tonight. Think of it as a challenge."

"This is not kick-boxing," she said.

Carole Anne laughed again. "You're always beating me at that," she said. "And I'd like to see you squirm for once."

"Carole Anne."

"Call him tonight," she said.

Valentine kept walking, oblivious to the argument happening around him. "Fine," she said. "I'll call him tonight."

A couple of hours later, she sat on her back deck, thank you very much, and clutched her phone in tight fingers. It was barely five o'clock, and she wondered if Dylan was even off of work yet.

Her backyard could probably be mowed one more time before autumn took completely over, and she thought about doing that. Maybe weeding the north side of the house. Maybe going down to the animal shelter and getting a dog.

Anything to keep herself busy until it was too late to call Dylan.

All at once, an idea hit her. "The church." There was always something going on over at the red brick building on the weekends. Even if it was the knitting club, it would keep her fingers busy, keep them away from the phone icon on her screen.

Why was it so hard for her to admit she *wanted* to call Dylan? She lifted her phone and tapped on the texts they'd exchanged. She sure liked texting better than calling, but he'd called her and she felt like she owed him more of a response.

So she tapped on the call icon and lifted the phone to her ear.

CHAPTER SEVEN

Lord Vader barked on the other side of the door, and Boone's muted chuckle came through the door. A second later, the door swung in and Lord Vader, a very solid yellow lab, came barreling onto the porch, his whip-like tail whapping against the porch railing and then Dylan's leg.

"Hey, buddy. Hey." Dylan laughed as he scrubbed the dog down. He glanced up at Boone. "Cubs tonight." He lifted the six-pack of Mountain Dew he'd brought. "It's been a long week. I think I might drink all of these myself."

Boone stepped back, his eyes searching Dylan's. "Rough week? I thought you won the Saddleback bid."

"I did." Dylan stepped into Boone's house, Lord Vader right at his side. The dog panted, perpetually wearing a smile that Dylan couldn't resist. He felt all the negativity that had been swirling inside his mind and staining his mood lift away. Maybe he should get a dog.

Then he'd have to move, as his building didn't allow pets. Dylan thought, not for the first time, that perhaps it was time for him to settle down. Buy a house. Find someone to live in it with him.

His job was pretty stable now, especially after Asher had said he'd train Dylan through every aspect of his duties, and Dylan sighed as he put the soda on Boone's kitchen counter.

"So why the rough week?"

Dylan gave his best friend a look and reached for a piece of all-meat pizza. "My mom said to invite you to dinner on Sunday."

"Can—?"

"Yes, Nicole is invited." Dylan tried not to sound upset about it. He wasn't, not really. He went into the living room and sat on the couch. Boone followed with the entire pizza box and all the soda.

"So this is a woman problem," he said as he sat on the other end of the couch. The baseball game Dylan had come to watch was already on the TV in front of them.

Dylan had never kept his dating disasters a secret from Boone, and he didn't see a reason to this time either. "Yeah, this is a woman problem." He slid a glance at Boone, who cracked the lid on a can of soda with a crackling *hiss!*

"I sort of, maybe, went out with Camila Cruz earlier this week."

Boone tried to breathe while he was drinking, which resulted in a coughing choke that took several seconds for him to clear from his throat. "Dude, some warning would've been nice." He wiped the front of his shirt, where some soda had spilled. "This is a new shirt."

"I said it was a woman problem." Dylan handed him another paper towel, a bit of amusement running through him at Boone's stained shirt.

Boone tossed the paper towel down. "How do you 'sort of, maybe' go out with someone?"

"She took my number, wouldn't give me hers, and hasn't texted or called me since." Dylan sighed and slumped back into the couch. "I did call her, but just got her voicemail."

"How long has this been going on?" Boone swiped off the cowboy hat he wore all the time and ran his fingers through his hair before putting it back on.

"Since Tuesday."

"And I'm just hearing about it?"

"I didn't want to bother you."

"Dylan," Boone said in his *not-this-again* voice. But instead of telling him he was welcome anytime, that Nicole didn't mind, blah blah blah, he said, "I thought you didn't like Camila Cruz. She's the plumber, right?"

"I don't, I mean, yeah, she's the plumber, and she's...." Truth was, he'd never looked Cami's way because of their first altercation. But maybe he'd misjudged her. Maybe he simply thought she was pretty.

"You like her," Boone said. "When did that happen?"

"Maybe on Monday?" Dylan guessed. "I don't know. She was putting in a bid when I was, and she was the only friendly face there, and...I just—I haven't been able to stop thinking about her since."

Boone handed him a can of soda. "So you *maybe* went out with her on Tuesday, when you won the bid."

"She won too, for Rogers Plumbing."

"Oh, good for them."

Boone was completely missing the point. "We have nothing in common." He heard the words in her voice, and the soda tasted like weak tea. "She even said so, and today, at the build site, she was all crabby with me. Like we hadn't even driven to Amarillo, or eaten her gourmet veggie-only pizza, or held hands on the way back."

"Whoa, hand-holding on the first date."

Dylan ignored him. He'd always moved faster than Boone had—at least until he'd met Nicole. Boone had fallen fast then.

He stared at the TV, not even seeing who was up to bat or who was pitching. He wasn't sure how Cami had penetrated his life so quickly. First, he was giving up meat on pizza and now he didn't care about baseball.

"Maybe you should call her," Boone said.

Was he not listening? "I already have. She didn't answer, nor did she call back." He popped the K on the last word, proud of himself for using a word like "nor" too.

"You have an emergency after-hours number for the plumber. Who do you think answers that?" Boone reached for his laptop, which sat on the coffee table where Dylan rested his feet.

"I don't know," Dylan said.

"Let's find out." Boone clicked and typed, a smile taking over his whole face in a way that Dylan found half annoying and half hopeful.

He turned the computer toward Dylan. "One way to find out."

"I'm not calling that." Dylan looked at the screen though,

the numbers right there for their twenty-four-hour service line.

"Your loss," Boone said, stretching his feet out in front of him and focusing on the TV. He even closed the laptop and put it on the coffee table. "I really hate the Cubs."

"Yeah, me too," Dylan said, his thoughts still revolving around Cami and sneaking through a back door to talk to her tonight.

He didn't notice the outs, the strikes, the home runs. Nothing. Maybe an hour passed before Boone said, "Call her. You're no fun when you're not even paying attention to the game." He stood up and stretched. "You want to keep the dogs?"

"What?" Dylan glanced up at him.

"I've asked you about ten questions." Boone grinned at him. "Call. Her." He fished his keys out of his pocket. "And keep Vader for a couple of nights." He started for the door.

"Wait." Dylan jumped to his feet and followed his best friend toward the exit. "Are we going out to Three Rivers tomorrow?"

"I'm renovating the back room of the animal hospital." He rolled his eyes. "The city provided the funding and says it needs to be done by the new year. Nicole and I are just getting it done as fast as we can."

"All right," Dylan said, wondering if Cami ever rode a horse. Being from Amarillo and all, she'd surely be at least a bit familiar with the animals.

Boone left, and Dylan really couldn't concentrate after that. All he wanted to do was hear Cami's voice and sit across from her as she told him about the old specs and how so much of her time had been wasted.

His heart squeezed. He'd have been so mad if he'd been operating on outdated plans and lost the time he could've used to take care of other jobs.

"Come on, buddy," he said to the dog. "Let's go for a walk." He leashed Vader and snuck him down the stairwell and out onto the street, leaving his phone sitting on the coffee table.

He made it about a block before he wanted to go back. While autumn had arrived, the air was still oppressively hot and while Dylan didn't mind hard work, he also didn't appreciate walking dogs.

"Oh, they're so cute," a woman said, causing Dylan to blink to focus on the one in front of him.

She crouched down in front of Vader, who licked her face as if she were a delicious ice cream cone. But Dylan knew Ebony Price, and she was only sweet to a point—usually until she found out how much money someone had.

She'd never targeted Dylan, and he wondered if she really was just happening by or not. She straightened, and she was wearing workout clothing—yoga pants and a tight lycra tank top. Her hair was back in a ponytail, and earbuds dangled from her ears.

Pulling them out, she said, "What's his name?"

"Vader." Dylan looked at her, trying to be attracted to Ebony, at least a little bit.

He felt nothing.

He wanted to call Cami now, more badly than ever. "Come on, Vader," he said, pulling on the dog's leash. "We've got to go." He put as much kindness into his smile as he could. "Sorry, just getting him out for a minute before I meet someone."

"Oh, okay." Ebony played with the end of her ponytail and didn't move out of his way. So Dylan turned around and went back toward his apartment, every step urging him to go faster and get back to his phone quicker.

"You can't have that animal in here," Mrs. Charles called to him from down the hall as he hurried Vader toward his apartment.

"I'm just here for a minute," he called back, fumbling with the doorknob. Inside his apartment, he filled a bowl with cold water for Vader and picked up his phone to check if he'd missed any messages or calls.

Of course he hadn't. Why did he want to talk to Cami so badly when she obviously didn't feel the same?

"One way to find out," he said, echoing something Boone had said earlier. Dylan flipped open his laptop and punched in the number for the after-hours plumbing line, hoping he wasn't making the biggest mistake of his life.

CHAPTER EIGHT

Cami's phone rang with the *tweet-twirp!* of a forwarded call. Someone's toilet was out on a Friday night. Great. Just great.

She sighed as she reached for the phone on the edge of the bathtub, where she'd retreated after chickening out and not even letting her phone connect to Dylan's.

"Rogers Plumbing," she said in the most business-like voice she could muster while in a bubble bath.

"You're kind of hard to track down, you know that?"

Cami's heart beat triple-time and water sloshed as she sat straight up. "Dylan?"

"I have a leak at my place," he said, his voice on the outer edge of flirtatious.

She relaxed back into the tub, a smile playing with her mouth too. "You do not."

He sighed, any playfulness that had been there before gone now. "No, I don't. I just...hey, so what happened today?"

Cami pressed her eyes closed as the way she'd treated him replayed behind her closed lids. She'd been a jerk today, that was what had happened. But she'd wasted half her day digging those wells, and the rental fee for the excavator had been several hundred dollars. Several hundred dollars she couldn't get back.

Still, she needed to learn how to control her temper. "I'm sorry," she said. "That wasn't my finest moment." She started to slip in the tub and she sat up, pushing the water dangerously close to her device.

"What was that noise?" he asked.

"Nothing." Her face heated at the very thought of him knowing she was in the tub. "This was an emergency call, you know."

"I was in crisis."

"Oh?"

"I...miss you."

Cami didn't know what to say. He couldn't possibly miss her. They'd barely spent any time together before the bid on Monday, and they'd gone to dinner once. For a few hours.

She shook her head, though that didn't translate over the phone. He couldn't possibly miss her. Could he?

"What are you doing tonight?" he asked.

She glanced down at the bubbles drifting across the surface of her bathwater. "Nothing."

"Want to do nothing with me?"

She did, but not this kind of nothing. "I need a few minutes to get ready." More than a few, but maybe he wasn't available—

"I'm on my way over."

"I—no—" But the line had gone dead, leaving her in the bathtub holding the phone.

A beat of silence filled the bathroom, the house, her soul. Then she flew into action, standing in one swift motion and sending water flowing over the edge of the tub and onto the floor. She nearly went down when she stepped onto the wet tile, but she gripped the vanity and managed to keep herself upright.

Her hair dripped down her back, and she needed a lot more than a few minutes to be ready, especially if she was going to go anywhere with a man. Let alone Dylan, who was a man among men.

Thinking fast, she wrapped herself in a towel and used the only thing she had to buy herself some time: her phone.

She'd wanted to text Dylan every night after work since their date on Tuesday. She'd turned the device off to keep herself from staying up all night, texting and giggling like a teenager.

She texted him now, though. *I need thirty minutes to be ready.*

And even that was a stretch with the current state of her hair—and her house. Should she invite him to come in? Make him wait in his truck? It did have leather seats....

Maybe I can meet you somewhere?

Fact or false: you're blowing me off.

False. I just need more time to be ready. I'll meet you anywhere you want.

Downtown park. We can walk around the duck pond. I'll bring you something.

Her stomach fell at what he'd bring. A dog? A sandwich?

Something could be *any*thing, but Cami couldn't dwell on that right now. She had an outfit to choose and hair to dry and the exact right pair of shoes to find for walking around the duck pond.

Fact: She needed more than thirty minutes.

But she couldn't be late, so she flung open her closet door and reached for the clothes closest to her.

She left her house forty minutes later, which meant she was already late to meet Dylan at the downtown pond. Didn't matter. Ten minutes later, she found him sitting on a bench on the edge of the park, a leashed yellow lab panting at his feet.

"Hey," she rushed forward, glad she'd gone with the more sensible footwear of her white leather sandals. She'd paired them with a pair of white shorts and a navy blue blouse. She'd managed to pull her hair into a low, slicked ponytail so it didn't matter that some of it was still damp.

"Aren't you a sight for sore eyes?" He stood and moved toward her, taking her right into his arms. He dipped his head and inhaled. "Mm, you smell like my favorite kind of soap."

She couldn't help the giggle that escaped her lips. "What kind of soap is that?"

"Whatever kind you use." He pulled back and grinned at her, taking her hand in one of his and picking up the dog's leash with the other.

"One of Boone's?" she asked.

"This is Lord Vader, and yeah, he belongs to Boone. He lets me take him when I'm—" He cut off suddenly, and Cami looked at him to find him gazing across the grass. "He lets me take him sometimes." Dylan ducked his head, a vulnerability about him that made Cami see a side of him she hadn't before.

She'd seen it on Tuesday too. It was the vulnerability, the softness of him, that had prompted her to maintain her distance. She could see herself falling for him way too fast, and that simply couldn't happen.

At least she didn't think it could, but as they strolled in the setting sun, finally reaching the duck pond on the far end of the park. With the water glinting on their left, and the soft panting sound of a dog beside them, she wondered why she couldn't be with him.

They didn't work together. She wouldn't lose her job if they broke up.

Maybe it's time to think about dating again, she thought. She'd been so closed off to the idea, it took a long time for the door to open, and even when it did, a loud, creaking sound reverberated through her mind.

"It cost me six-ninety-five to rent that excavator," she said, breaking the silence between them. "Well, not me, but the Rogers's. And they don't have seven hundred dollars to spare. I was...angry. Frustrated. I didn't mean to take it out on you." She peered up at him, hoping he'd forgive her. Understand that sometimes she just had a very short fuse, and she never knew what was going to light it.

"I know," he said simply, his fingers tightening for half a heartbeat. "I'm just glad there was no jukebox involved this time."

Her heart froze as if someone had doused it in liquid nitrogen. "I—"

Dylan laughed, the joyful sound lifting into the sky and making Cami smile despite herself. He let go of her hand and put his arm around her shoulders, tucking her into his side.

"You're full of fire," he said, leaning closer. His lips skimmed her earlobe when he said, "Don't worry. I'm not afraid of getting burned."

Fireworks popped through her whole body, and she had no idea what to say.

Didn't matter. Dylan seemed stuffed full of words tonight where he'd been quiet on Tuesday, let her lead the conversation where she wanted it to go.

And she had been rude to him when she'd first got to town. He'd tried to approach her at the jukebox in the diner, and she remembered vaguely speaking to him in Spanish, a lot of glaring, and then marching away.

He'd had no idea she'd just gotten off the phone with her ex, nor that she'd just decided she wouldn't be going back to Amarillo—ever.

She should probably explain all of that, but he didn't seem to need it.

"Fact or false," he said. "You haven't dated since you moved to Three Rivers."

She wondered who he'd been talking to. Boone Carver wouldn't know. Cami didn't have any pets, and she had no reason to go into the animal clinic.

"Fact," she said, drawing out the word. Maybe his sisters had told him. He had three of them, and they could mobilize the gossip circles and find out anything they wanted to know in minutes.

"Why's that?" he asked.

"I had a bad experience with my last boyfriend," she said, going for the truth. They rounded the pond on the far end, and the scent of freshly moved grass and sunshine filled the air.

"Tell me about it," he said, almost a question but not quite.

Cami contemplated her options. She'd been carrying the weight of what had gone down with Wade for a long time. Too long.

"His name was Wade," she started. "He was my boss's son. He was...abusive."

Dylan's next step took him away from her, and he looked fully at her, his eyes wide and round. "Physically?"

She nodded, the evening sun suddenly too cold. "I—I didn't have the fire then that I do now."

"Cami." His voice carried more emotion than Cami had heard in a long time. She realized in that moment how lonely she'd become, how isolated. Sure, she was strong but it sure would be nice to be weak sometimes. Have someone support her when she didn't feel like she could make it through another day.

"That's not okay," he said. "How long did that go on?"

"Too long," she said. "Months. I was afraid of him, and I knew I'd lose my job, so...."

"What was the turning point?"

"He was careful about not leaving a mark, until he wasn't. I couldn't go visit my parents, couldn't go to church, couldn't go to work." Cami took a deep breath, remembering the moment she'd decided to leave Wade, leave Amarillo, leave that old life behind. It was as clear as glass, right there in her memory to be thought of at any time.

"I...snapped or something. I don't know. But I didn't hide out in my apartment the way I usually did. I went to my parents' house. And church. And work. And anyone who asked what had happened, I told them the truth." She shook her head. "I quit that morning, and I left Amarillo that evening. I don't go back very often." Except to take him to her favorite pizza joint. Cami realized the significance of that date, and there was no doubt in her mind now that she liked this man standing in front of her.

Dylan took several steps, the information clearly needing some time to sink in. Finally, he said, "It doesn't seem fair that you had to leave."

"Tell me about it."

"So you don't see your family often?"

"Not that often, no." She thought of the simple hour-long drive—the house right next door where her former boss lived. No, she didn't go home very often.

"And you're still game for my family barbecue?" he asked. "Because they can be a handful."

"Did you ask your sisters about my dating history?"

"Did you ask your girlfriends about mine?"

She gave him a genuine smile. "So Kacey wasn't right about everything."

"So my sisters were." He shrugged. "Doesn't really matter to me."

"Nothing seems to," she said.

That made him pause, and he stepped in front of her. "What does that mean?"

"It means, Mister, that you're so calm and cool about everything." She swatted his chest. "It's unnerving."

He dodged away from her next swipe, latching onto her wrist with his strong, capable hands. "Unnerving, huh?" He switched his gaze from her fingers to her face. "You unnerve me too, Cami."

Before she could comprehend what he'd said or what he was doing, he bent toward her, her wrist still deliciously encircled by his fingers.

Her eyes drifted closed in anticipation of getting kissed, but his lips bypassed hers and landed on her cheek, near her eye. "I was wondering," he said softly, his next kiss closer to her ear. "Do you happen to know how to ride a horse?"

Cami's eyes jerked open, and she startled away from him. "Really?"

"I love going out to Three Rivers Ranch," he said, an insane amount of hope in his eyes. "I volunteer with the veterans at Courage Reins a couple of times a week, but I was thinking maybe me and you…I mean, you and I, we could go riding together or something."

"Are you kidding me right now?" Cami felt like she'd just arrived at the best surprise party in the world.

He sighed. "I guess we'll just keep searching for the one thing we have in common."

She stepped with him, making him wait just a little bit longer. "Oh, I don't think we'll need to do that," she finally said. "Because if there's one thing I like better than chocolate cake, it's horseback riding."

"Really?" Dylan asked.

"Really." She laughed, and he swung her around as he chuckled too.

"Well, that's just great, sweetheart," he said. "Want to go out to the ranch tomorrow?"

Cami's joy faded as quickly as it had lifted, but she didn't want to push him away anymore, so she said, "I do. I really do."

CHAPTER NINE

*D*ylan set Cami on her feet and gazed down at her, a range of happiness and affection racing through him. The moment lengthened, as she looked back at him with those gorgeous eyes.

So he'd been prolonging the moment before he kissed her, but now the idea came back in full color. Before he could lean down, he became aware of the pressure of Lord Vader's body against his calf and the hot, wet sensation of the dog's saliva as it dripped onto his toes. Dylan pulled away again but kept Cami as close as he could as he glanced down at the dog. "Vader." He gave the dog a little nudge.

He couldn't believe that an hour ago he was slumped on his couch, his heart heavy and his mind churning. Everything had changed when she'd walked up to him, her smile bright, her tone flirtatious, her curves so dang pronounced in that tiny scrap of fabric she called a pair of shorts.

And they were white, which only made her tan legs seem

to go on for miles and miles. Dylan reined in his thoughts and tucked Cami against his chest. He tried not to notice how easily she went, how well she fit. But he noticed. He noticed hard.

"How about some ice cream?" he asked, taming his fantasies and realizing the moment had passed. "The shop's just back that way."

"Yeah, it's like four blocks back that way."

"Oh, you don't want to walk?" he teased. "I'll drive you."

"That would be great, thanks." She flashed him a flirtatious smile that had him thinking about how he'd been too slow making his way toward her mouth for a kiss.

They walked back around the duck pond, Dylan thinking of one of his favorite childhood treats—pistachio ice cream. "My dad brought us for ice cream every weekend," Dylan said, not really sure why he was sharing this deeply personal part of his life with Cami, a woman he sure liked a lot but didn't know really well.

"Me and my sisters. We'd get ice cream cones every weekend, skip rocks right here in this pond, and then Dad would let us get a waffle to share before we went home." He thought of how he'd always had to run to keep up with his older, longer-legged sisters, how he always got the last cone from the counter, how he barely got two bites of waffle before Alecia would whisk the treat away from him.

"We got to spend time with Dad," he said. "It was fun."

"Sounds fun. We can go. I know they have ice cream sandwiches made with homemade cookies."

"Those aren't homemade, you know."

"Yes, they are." She glanced at him. "It says so right on the sign."

He glanced at her, pressed his lips together, and shook his head. "I happen to know they buy them from Cisco. Same ones you get at the burger joint."

Cami blinked a few times like she'd been personally affronted. "Well, I still like them."

Of course she did. Dylan was starting to get used to the fact that no matter what he liked, she wouldn't, and what she liked, he probably didn't.

Not a big deal, he thought. They seemed to get along okay, and their bodies were definitely in a perfect partnership during that almost kiss....

And she liked horseback riding, so that was a huge win in Dylan's book.

He helped her into the truck, thinking that her perfume would get trapped in the cab and he'd be able to smell her there. He drove down the road at a crawl, wanting her in his truck for a bit longer.

Once inside the ice cream shop, he ordered a pistachio ice cream cone for him and a "homemade" ice cream sandwich for her. Once they were back outside with Lord Vader shuffling along beside them, he said, "Let me prep you about my family. I'll tell them about you before we go. I should probably tell my mom this week, as she'll probably need extra time to make another batch of potato salad."

A beat of silence passed, and then Cami said, "You're kidding, right?"

"Not even a little bit." Dylan chuckled at the thought of his petite, blonde mother. "She plans everything down to the smallest detail. She makes *binders* of her plans. So me adding a girlfriend to the picture will upset her seating arrangements, her food—"

"Girlfriend?" Cami stopped, the hand holding her ice cream freezing in mid-air.

Dylan licked his ice cream, waiting for the playful smile. It didn't come, and frustration bolted through him.

"I was about to kiss you back there, Camila. What do you think is going on here?" Dylan lowered his cone and watched her. Watched the pure fear roll across her face. Watched a blush stain her cheeks.

He leaned over and pressed his mouth against her blush on the right, and then the left. "Don't answer that, okay?" He stepped back and started walking again. "I won't call you my girlfriend when I tell my mom."

She caught up to him, but she didn't say anything. Just licked the edge of her ice cream sandwich and then bit it, one ruby-red lip on each side. Dylan wanted to kiss her very badly, taste the chocolate and vanilla on her tongue, mess that lipstick up a little.

He looked away and caged his fantasies. She didn't even want to be called his girlfriend, and while he'd thought she'd definitely let him kiss her while they were alone in the park, it was obviously a different matter being called his while in a group of people. His family.

"We've only been out twice," she said when they reached his truck. "*Girlfriend* is just a little fast for me."

"All right," Dylan said, hoping some of that calm, coolness she'd accused him of earlier had infused his voice. He flashed her a smile, thinking *I don't need the label right now. I like her. She obviously likes me. That's enough.*

"How about lunch tomorrow?" he asked. "And then we can go out to the ranch."

"I eat lunch," she said, which caused Dylan to laugh.

He threaded his fingers through hers again, enjoying the sensation of her skin against his and the scent of that soap on her neck.

∽

THE FOLLOWING MORNING, DYLAN STOPPED BY HIS MOM and dad's before his lunch date with Cami.

"Mom," he called as he pushed into the red brick rambler.

"In the garden," came the reply.

He went past the steps leading upstairs, where his childhood bedroom still held football trophies and his old baseball mitt. His father sat at the kitchen counter, doing something on his tablet. "Hey, Dad." Dylan didn't even slow down as he pushed the sliding glass door farther open and stepped into the backyard.

"Hey, Ma." He leaned over and gave her a quick kiss on top of her head. She stood and gave him a hug, patting him on the back.

"How are you?" She stepped back and brushed her hands together. "What are you doing here?"

Dylan couldn't stop the smile spreading across his face. "I came to let you know I'm bringing a woman to the barbecue."

Shock painted his mother's face, which also broke into a grin. "A woman? Troy!"

"Oh, Dad doesn't need to know," Dylan said too late, as his father appeared in the doorway.

"What?" he asked.

"Dylan's bringing someone to the barbecue."

"In three weeks," Dylan said. "We might break up by then." He didn't mention that Cami wasn't even his girlfriend. They were definitely dating; she couldn't deny that. Well, she probably could. Dylan didn't want to think about it.

"Oh, Dylan." His mother slapped him with her gardening gloves. "What's her name?"

"Camila Cruz."

"The plumber?" his dad asked.

"Yep." Dylan grinned. "We both won the bid at the new housing project going in up north."

"You won the bid?" His mom shrieked and threw herself into his arms.

Dylan laughed. "Mom, I work for the city, remember?"

"You worked hard on that bid."

He had worked hard on that bid, so he took their congratulations and even let his mom text all his sisters with him standing right there.

"I have to go," he said a few minutes later, after his dad had poured him sweet tea and his mother had asked him if he wanted a breakfast sandwich. He'd declined, but he'd thought seriously about saying yes. His mother was the best cook in the county, maybe even the whole state of Texas. Her fried egg breakfast sandwiches could bring in a mass of people, but Dylan wanted to be hungry when he went to lunch with Cami.

"Stop by tonight," his mom implored as she walked him to the door. "Sally's coming with the kids because Hugh is out of town. I'm making sausage Alfredo pizza."

Dylan's stomach roared at the thought of that pizza. "I'll tell Boone too."

"Yes." His mother's eyes sparkled as if she hadn't had anyone to cook for in years. "Tell him to bring Nicole."

Dylan waved and headed out the front door, his thumbs sending the message to Boone. He'd bring Nicole, and for the first time in a while, Dylan's jealousy didn't rear up. He smiled and headed over to the older section of town, where Cami lived.

He passed the church and decided to swing into the parking lot real quick. He felt worlds out of his league with Cami, with the upcoming build, with taking his girlfriend—whether she wanted to be called that or not—to meet his family in three short weeks.

And he needed a little divine intervention. It seemed impossible that he hadn't had the opportunity to attend church since the dinner with Cami. If he had, he wouldn't feel so out of sorts.

He gazed up at the steeple on the church and took a moment to close his eyes. Breathe. Just breathe.

Help me with Camila Cruz, he prayed. He didn't need a powerful feeling to overcome him. Prayer worked inside him, and it always made him feel better even if he never got a definitive answer.

But he felt more peaceful about his upcoming day, and his excitement for lunch and horseback riding returned.

"Thank you," he verbalized as he backed out of the parking space and turned back onto the road. He drove toward her house, enjoying the lazy breeze and low traffic on this Saturday.

He pulled into the driveway of a small, white house that had a big porch that spanned the whole front and wrapped around both corners.

Rose bushes lined either side of the front steps, and a wind chime hung from the eaves. Her door was painted a nice shade of mint green, and the trees in this neighborhood were mature and tall, casting the houses in shade.

Dylan thought it absolutely fit Cami, and he waved to a blonde woman as he got out of his truck and started toward the door. Then he did a double-take. "Carole Anne?"

"Dylan Walker," she said with a huge grin. "So she called you, huh?"

Dylan paused while still on the sidewalk and looked at her. "Uh, what?"

Carole Anne got up and started across the patch of lawn that separated the two properties. "She didn't call you?"

"Nope." He shook his head and accepted a quick hug from her. "How's Levi? Things so exciting at the bank?" Dylan couldn't imagine being cooped up in an office, wearing a suit and tie to work each day. But hey, he supposed there was a job for everyone.

"So exciting," Carole Anne said. "So if she didn't call you, why are you here?"

He leaned in close, a smile touching his mouth. "I called the emergency plumbing line. She *had* to answer."

Carole Anne pealed out a laugh, and Dylan chuckled too. "Well, good for you," she said. "Sometimes Cami can be a bit prickly."

"Really?" Dylan asked as he started up the steps. "I hadn't noticed."

CHAPTER TEN

Cami primped in the mirror, trying to get one curl to go in the right direction. Why it wouldn't was making her frustrated, and she slicked her fingers through her pomade one more time.

The doorbell rang, and her hand jerked, making the curl even more ridiculous. And completely going the wrong direction now.

"Whatever," she muttered to herself. She pressed her lips together, satisfied with the dark purple stain and the way it played with her skin.

She moved the few steps down the hall and through the living room to the door. A quick exhale and she pulled open the door to find the best looking, single man in town standing on her doorstep.

Hers.

Her lungs forgot how to breathe, especially when he

smiled at her. "Hey, there," he said, and Cami managed to grin back at him.

"Hey," she said. "You want to come in for a minute? Get the grand tour?"

"Sure." Dylan eased into her personal space, easily slipping his hand along her waist and moving past her without being too handsy.

But wow, she wanted him to be a little more handsy. He smelled like the woods and fresh air, and he wore a plain gray T-shirt with a pair of jeans that shouldn't make a man look so good.

"This is nice," he said, glancing around.

"The house is ninety-four-years-old," she said, her nerves infusing into her voice. She gave an anxious laugh and pointed to the fireplace. "But I built that mantel just last year."

"You did?" Dylan moved over to it and ran his fingers along it. "It's nice. What kind of wood?"

"It was reclaimed from the barn out at the Lawrence's place. Have you been out there?"

"Yeah, sod farm, right?" He turned back to her, so cool, so calm, so cute.

"Right." She slicked her sweaty palms down her jeans. "So it's kind of small, but it's just me, so it's not bad." Her front room was only big enough for a couch, not a set, but she'd managed to cram in a recliner too. "Kitchen's back here."

She moved past the hall that led to the bathroom—the only bathroom—and the two bedrooms—and into the kitchen. "Dine-in eating," she said. "I have a table on the deck out back too. Sometimes I eat out there."

Cami went outside, because the galley kitchen was way too small for her and Dylan—at least if she didn't want to "accidentally" trip into him and press her lips to his.

She sighed once outside, but her internal temperature was off the charts, and being outside at noon didn't help. The shade would shift as the sun moved, but for now, the backyard was in full sun.

Dylan joined her, and he said, "Yeah, this is great."

"You sound like you really like it." She surveyed the backyard and wasn't all that impressed. The garden in the corner hadn't been planted in years, as she didn't have time, but she did manage to keep the lawn and bushes the previous owner had planted alive.

"I do," he said, slipping his hand into hers. "I don't have a yard or a deck or a front porch." He cut a glance at her out of the side of his eye, but she wasn't sure if he was glad he didn't have those things or not. "I've actually been thinking about getting a more permanent place."

"Your apartment isn't permanent?"

"I mean, yeah, sure it is. I guess." He shrugged. "I just feel like maybe I should be a real adult."

She squeezed his hand. "I think you're a real adult. People live in apartments, Dylan."

He met her eye, and a powerful moment bloomed between then. "I'd like to get a dog," he said, his mouth barely moving and his eyes dropping to her painted lips. "And I can't have them in the building."

"Better move then." She bumped him with her hip. "And I'm starving, so let's go." She led him back into the house and paused at the mouth of the hallway. "Bedrooms and bathroom down there. Nothing fancy."

"And land," he said. "For horses. I'd like that too. A big garden."

Cami grinned at the wistful joy in his voice. "Do you actually have time to work in a garden?"

"Well, no, but I do like eating fresh peas. In fact, we used to invade Old Man Mission's garden every spring. He finally started planting four extra rows of peas and labeling them 'For the Thieves'." He chuckled and moved to her side as they walked down the steps.

"I actually feel bad about that now."

"Yeah, I don't think so." She giggled, and the sound felt strange coming out of her mouth. "Where are we going for lunch?"

"Where do you want to go for lunch?"

"Have fun, you two," Carole Anne called, and Cami startled toward her.

"Oh, hey," she said, heat shooting into her face. "You know Dylan."

"Already talked to him on the way in." Carole Anne twirled one of her perfect curls around her fingers, wearing a knowing look on her face. "He told me all about his plumbing emergency last night. Good thing you were there to help him."

"Oh, uh, right," she said. "And you win, okay?"

"I totally did." Carole Anne beamed at her, and Dylan shifted beside her. "See you at kick-boxing on Monday morning. You're buying the coffee after."

"That wasn't part of the deal."

"It is now," Carole Anne said, her smile as wide as the whole state.

Cami turned back to Dylan, his curiosity plain on his face. "I'll tell you about it later. I really am starving."

He led her to his truck and opened the door for her. Once he got behind the wheel, he asked, "So where to? You never said."

Cami looked across the bench seat at him, wondering if she should've slid over and sat immediately beside him. That was what cowgirl girlfriends did, wasn't it?

But she couldn't do it now, and she gave him a quick smile, trying to remember the question. "Oh, lunch." She took in a big breath. "There's a new bistro over by the steakhouse. Have you been there?"

"I don't even know what a bistro is." He flipped the truck into reverse and backed out of her driveway. "What kind of food do they have?"

"Sandwiches, soups, salads, awesome desserts."

"Well, that sounds great." He glanced at her. "I like desserts."

Cami kept her eyes on him, an internal war starting inside her brain. Back and forth she went for a block, and then she said, "After I moved out of my parents' house, I ate dessert at every meal, and always first."

"Is that so?" Dylan's voice carried plenty of flirt. "What kind of dessert?"

"My favorite is chocolate cake," she said. "With plenty of chocolate frosting." Her mouth watered just thinking about it.

"And chocolate chips?" he asked.

She made a face. "Definitely not," she said. "Cake should melt in your mouth, not be chewed."

"No chocolate chips. Got it." His phone rang, and he glanced at it on the seat beside him. "Oh, this is Bill Owens. I have to take it. Okay?" He looked at her for permission, and she waved her hand.

Instead of picking up the phone, he pressed a button on his steering wheel. "Hey, Bill. You're on speaker in my truck. Cami Cruz is with me." He smiled at her.

"Okay," Bill said. "I'm calling about the Christmas parade."

"Yeah," Dylan said. "Yep." He'd obviously been expecting the call.

"I know you won the bid up at Rivers Merge, but will you still have time to do the wiring for us?"

"Of course," Dylan said. "Absolutely."

"Great." The relief in Bill's voice wasn't hard to find. "So I'm wondering how packed your day is...."

Dylan looked at Cami, and she really wanted to see how this would play out. "I'm headed to lunch right now," he said cautiously. "And then out to Three Rivers. But depending on what you need, I could stop by in between."

"The sleigh is on Seventeenth Street, and it needs a jump. However, Tanya is afraid to do it, because the battery looks corroded. She wants you to check it out before they try to move it."

Dylan glanced at Cami again and pressed another button. "Are you up for jump-starting a sleigh?"

"You wire the Christmas parade?"

"Every year."

As if Cami didn't have enough reasons to like him. "I'd love to jump-start a sleigh before we head out to the ranch."

He pressed the button again, and said, "Bill? I can be there in about an hour. Sound good?"

"See you then."

Dylan seemed to enjoy the roast beef panini at the bistro, though he claimed to have never eaten a pressed sandwich before.

Their conversation had been easy, with updates about his family as he prepared her to meet his family in a couple of weeks, and talk about the build and their jobs.

Cami really enjoyed herself, and as they pulled up to a giant sleigh on Seventeenth Street, she couldn't wait to see him in action.

"Sorry about this," he said as three people came out of the house where the sleigh was and came down the sidewalk toward them. "You want to sit in the sleigh?"

"Heck, yeah, I do." Cami unbuckled her seat belt and got out, braving the heat to see the sleigh up close. One of her favorite things about Three Rivers was their Christmas traditions, and she'd loved the sleigh pulled by big Clydesdale horses, carrying Santa Claus and his giant sack of toys.

"Cami," Dylan said, meeting her near the corner of the truck. "This is Bill Owens. He organizes the Christmas parade."

"Nice to meet you." She shook his hand. "And Patricia Raines. She and her husband maintain and store all the vehicles here on their property on Seventeenth Street."

Cami nodded at her, smiling for all she was worth.

"And her daughter, Tanya."

"Nice to meet you all," she said.

"You work for Rogers Plumbing, don't you?" Patricia asked, a kindness to her voice that told Cami she shouldn't have holed herself up quite so much in Three Rivers. There were good people here.

"I do," she said. "Yes."

"Congrats on winning the bid up at Rivers Merge," Bill said, glancing at Dylan, who also wore a smile.

"Okay." Dylan clapped his hands. "Let's look at this sleigh." He moved around to the back of it, where a panel had been removed to reveal an engine.

"I thought the horses pulled the sleigh," she said.

"They do," Bill said. "But we can't hook it up to horses all the time. So it can drive itself when necessary."

"And the water in the runners require power," Patricia said.

"Water?" Cami glanced at her.

"It rarely snows here," she said. "So to make it easier for the horses to pull the sleigh down Main Street, we keep the runners wet so they slide easier."

"Oh." Cami had no idea so much went into the parade.

Dylan said, "Oh, yeah. This needs to be replaced." He straightened. "We can run over to the Super Smith and get a new battery." He met Cami's eyes, a silent question in his.

She nodded, because he was sexy while he worked, and the horses could wait. After all, there was still plenty of time for whatever they wanted to do.

"You guys don't need to wait for us," Dylan said. "I'll text you when I'm done."

"Thanks, Dylan," Bill said, and the three of them moved

back toward the house, Bill and Patricia already talking about other aspects of the parade.

"How long does it take you to do all the wiring?" she asked as they started toward the hardware store.

"Depends on how crazy Bill gets with the floats. The city owns about two dozen of them. We only pull out about ten every year. Some of them are more complicated than others."

"Ah, I see." She had seen different floats each year, though there were some staples like the sleigh.

He bought a battery, saying, "Put this on the city tab for the parade," as a way to pay, and twenty minutes later, everything with the sleigh was ready to go.

He brushed his hands together as if they were dirty, and Cami had never seen such a good-looking man. She wanted to throw herself into his arms and kiss him, but she wondered if that would be too forward.

And too soon, her mind screamed at her.

Then she reminded herself that she hadn't dated in four years. And she had a handsome, single, interested-in-her man standing right in front of her.

"Good job," she said, stepping up to him and running her fingers along the collar of his shirt.

He stilled, and their eyes met. She slowly, carefully, leaned into him and wrapped her arms around him.

"Oh, okay," he said, grinning. "Are we still going horseback riding?"

"Definitely," she said. "I just wanted to try something first."

"You want to jump-start the sleigh?" His gaze dropped to her mouth, and she shook her head.

She tipped up, and he leaned down, and all of her nerves fled when his lips touched hers. She didn't mind that they were standing in a very public place. Didn't mind that she didn't know everything about him. Didn't mind that they had very little in common.

Her mouth moved in sync with his in a way it never had with anyone else. She trailed her hands up his biceps to his shoulders and then into his hair.

He kissed her and kissed her, until she realized they definitely had something else in common: They liked to kiss each other.

CHAPTER ELEVEN

Dylan held onto the curves of Cami's hips, his pulse bouncing around in his chest like a ping pong ball. Up. Down. Left. Right. Diagonal.

The touch of the woman's fingers along his scalp sent fire everywhere, and he finally pulled back enough to separate them. "Dang," he whispered, his eyes opening slowly to see she still had hers closed. She pressed her lips together as if tasting him there, and he couldn't help himself. He kissed her again.

And she'd started it. Dylan couldn't believe it, though he had certainly been thinking about kissing Cami before this day ended.

He finally broke their connection, and he rested his forehead against hers. They breathed in tandem, and then she gave a light laugh.

She breathed out heavily, and said, "So horseback riding?"

"Yeah," he said. "Yep, let's go." He helped her into his

truck again and when he opened his door to get behind the wheel, she'd scooted across the bench seat so she could sit right next to him.

She linked her hand through his arm and rested her head on his bicep. "Tell me more about what you do at Courage Reins."

"So I go out on Tuesday and Thursday nights. Pete—he's the owner—lets me help the veterans get set-up on their horses. I talk to them, and just watch them work with the horses." He chuckled, because he knew the veterans came out for therapy, and that the horses helped them physically, as well as emotionally and spiritually.

But they did the same for him.

"I sometimes ride, and sometimes I just hang out on the fences. Sometimes Pete has treats, and sometimes I get to stay and eat with his family."

"Sounds nice," she said. "I almost always go out to ride Valentine at Brynn's stables on Friday nights."

"Really?" Dylan looked at her as he turned right onto the road that led out to the ranch.

"Really." She snuggled deeper into his side. "Just for a few hours. I love horses."

"Did your family have horses growing up?" he asked.

"No, but my best friend did. They had a whole boarding stable, and we'd ride every day after school." She sounded so happy, and Dylan wanted to know everything about her.

"My family had a few horses," he said. "My dad loves them, and he thought they'd teach us to work."

"And did they?"

"Oh, yeah. Had to get up before school and do chores.

Had to work in the hay fields. Horses required care." He said the last words in a deeper voice to emulate his father and added a chuckle. "Even the girls had farm chores."

"I just had my older brother," she said. "And he's several years older than me, so I was an only child for a while. I had to do everything."

"I'm the only boy," he said. "So I get that. My sisters—they're great—but they knew how to get out of anything and everything."

"I bet they did." She laughed, and Dylan liked the way it filled his cab.

"So, I just want to clear up all the...rumors," he said, glancing at her. She stiffened beside him, and he thought maybe he shouldn't ruin their near-perfect day.

But he wanted her to know everything about him too. "So I'm a pretty easy-going guy, and I guess a lot of women like that. For a while there, I liked having a date all the time."

"I really don't need to know," she said, straightening though she kept her arm linked through his. "You explained enough to me already."

"Did I?"

"Yeah, when you told me about the teacher at the pizzeria."

"I'm not a player," he said, needing to say the words. "I like to watch baseball with Boone, and I like to eat good food, and I like my family. I'm hoping to take over the Electric Company when Asher retires. He's teaching me."

"That's great, Dylan."

"So I know my life is kind of simple, but—"

"I like simple," she said, cutting him off. "You really don't need to make yourself look better. You're already great."

"Yeah? Is that why you kissed me in broad daylight on Seventeenth Street?"

"Your big head isn't your most attractive quality," she said dryly.

He chuckled and turned onto the dirt road that led to the ranch. "So do you only ride Valentine?"

"When I come out here? Yeah, just Valentine. Brynn and I sort of have an agreement."

"Okay, so I didn't know that," he said. "So I called Pete and I asked him if we could ride a couple of his horses, and he said yes. One of them is not Valentine."

"That's fine," she said with a giggle. "I can ride other horses."

"Great." Relief flowed through him as he pulled up to Courage Reins. Saturday was one of their busier days, but Pete had assured him they had horses to spare. He grabbed his cowboy hat from the backseat and positioned it on his head once he got out of the truck.

"Oh, wow," she said with a smile as he rounded the truck. "Look at you. All cowboy'ed up." She reached up and touched the brim of his hat.

"You like it, admit it." He added a bit of swagger to his walk.

She rolled her eyes, which made her different than the other women he'd ever dated. Which made him like her so much more than he already did.

"Are we going in?"

"Of course." He opened the door and waited for Cami to

walk through it. No one sat at the reception desk, where Reese usually did. So he took Cami's hand and led her past the desk and out to the stables.

"He said we can take any horses that are in a stall. Oh, look, Mint Brownie is available. I love him." He stepped over to the stall and stroked the horse's face. "You want to pick one?"

She wandered down the aisle away from him, and he called, "There are boots at the end there, if you want to wear some." He got the tack he needed and started saddling Mint Brownie.

He wasn't sure where Cami had gone, but when he led his horse out of the stall, he found her properly booted and leading a black horse named Oreo in front of her.

"Are all the horses named after foods here?" she asked.

"Most here, yeah," he said. "Obviously not over at Brynn's, though I don't get over there very much." Or ever, really. No wonder he didn't know Cami came out to the ranch to ride on Fridays.

Pete would never tell him such things. And as Chelsea had more kids, she'd dropped off on all the matchmaking. Still. He wondered if either of them would've set him up with Cami anyway. It wasn't exactly like they got along.

Then he remembered that kiss, and he thought he was doing just fine, thank you very much.

Outside, Cami swung effortlessly into the saddle and glanced over her shoulder. "We just go wherever we want?"

"Yeah," he said, mounting Mint Brownie and coaching the horse forward so they were side-by-side. "There's a nice stream about a half-hour ride out, if you want to go there."

She cast a glance over her shoulder. "I don't usually ride on this side of the ranch."

"Well, let's go then." And they set off for the river.

"So tell me more about your family," she said. "I think you've only gone over two sisters. The youngest is...?"

"Rose," he said. "And let me tell you, she's the easiest one, so I think you'll be fine."

∼

DYLAN PARKED IN THE LOT THE FOLLOWING MORNING, THE wonderful little church that brought him so much peace in front of him. He'd been brave when he'd dropped her off after horseback riding and asked Cami about sitting by him at the service today. She'd blinked—her only hesitation—and said yes.

He spotted her as he got out of his truck. She wore a sundress in a cacophony of colors and a pair of strappy blue sandals that inched her closer to his height. He strode across the distance between them and swept her into his arms. "Hey, pretty girl."

She grinned up at him. "Tie and everything." Cami flipped the turquoise tie his sister had given him for his birthday a few months ago.

"Dress and everything." He didn't flip the hem of her skirt though the thought flitted through his mind. "Come on, I think Boone is saving us a seat."

He sure was, and Dylan appreciated that he and Nicole sat near the back. "Hey, guys," he said. "This is Camila Cruz. Cami, this is Boone and Nicole."

Boone, ever the people's man, stood and shook Cami's hand, his perfect gentleman smile stuck in place. Nicole was a little more real, and she made room for Cami on the bench. They started talking, and Dylan sat on the end of the row, already anxious to leave.

He enjoyed church, really he did. Pastor Scott said great things, and the general vibe always left Dylan feeling better about his life. For some reason, today he was anxious behind walls. He wanted to get outside, even in the Texas heat, and figure some things out before he had to go over to his parents' for Sunday dinner alone.

Why did he have to go alone? He could ask Cami, and she'd probably come. She didn't go visit her family, and he'd learned yesterday at lunch that she often argued with her brother about fair wages for women working the same jobs as men.

Dylan liked her fire, every flame of it, and they'd talked a lot about her job as a plumber. She felt under-appreciated in her field, constantly judged, and like she had to be twice as tough as a male plumber would have to be.

Dylan couldn't speak to that or not. He didn't know her fight. Would never have to know it. So he'd held her hand and listened to her and hoped that would be enough.

"You want to come over after church?" she whispered, tucking her arm through his and sliding a bit closer to him.

And he found his way out of the family dinner he didn't want to attend alone. "Heck yes, I do."

She giggled and pressed her face into his arm to muffle the sound. When she calmed enough to speak again, she whispered, "I'm not much of a cook, but I can put together a pretty good grilled peanut butter and banana sandwich."

"Sounds amazing." Compared to the noise, the glances, and the endless questions he'd endure at his family dinner, a quiet afternoon kissing Cami sounded downright heavenly.

He focused on the pastor, who said, "...so don't despair, my friends. The Lord knows you, as you are right now. He knows where you've been. He knows where you're going, and He knows the best way to get you there." Pastor Scott surveyed the crowd as he let his words sink in.

"The real test is to see if you'll *let* Him lead you." The preacher smiled and placed both palms flat against the pulpit. "Let Him lead you, even if you think you know where you're going."

Dylan cocked his head, trying to find the meaning in the pastor's words. He seemed to be looking right at Dylan, though he couldn't possibly be doing so. Dylan knew where he was going—nowhere. At least not physically. He'd grown up in Three Rivers, and he loved it here. He had a great job that had some room to grow.

He glanced at Cami, sitting beside him. He could definitely use some guidance when it came to her. So he closed his eyes, almost an acquiescence of his own will, and prayed, *Help me to know what to say and do with Camila to keep her in my life.*

Because he liked her. He liked driving with her at his side, and riding a horse with her nearby. And while he'd felt a connection with other women, none of them were as hot as the one with Cami and he thought maybe she could be part of his grown-up life—if he didn't mess it up.

CHAPTER TWELVE

Monday morning, Cami studied the new specs she'd been given. She'd double- and then triple-checked to make sure they were the right ones before she did anything, planned anything, reserved any more equipment.

The phone rang, and she picked it up without looking away from the build schedule. "Rogers Plumbing."

"There's water all over in the high school gym and training room," a man said. That got Cami's attention, and she looked up from her specs. "Our sprinkler pipes have broken in the field above the school, and everything is a muddy mess."

"I'll be out there in ten minutes," Cami said. "Have you turned the water off?"

"Yes, all shut down."

"Great. See you in a few."

Broken sprinkler pipes didn't sound like an hour or two.

Oh, no. Cami knew this would be a week-long job—and she had a meeting with Saddleback's general contractor at one o'clock and two jobs to complete before then. She hurried out to Penny, thinking she'd just see how this morning went and make a phone call to reschedule things if she had to.

When she pulled into the high school parking lot and found the principal flagging her down from the west side—up the hill from the school—she knew the entire day would be spent here.

"A muddy mess" didn't even begin to cover what she saw before her. Swampland would be a better term. She put on her knee-high rubber boots and made her way out into the field, leaving the principal on the curb.

She had no idea what kind of pipes had been used in this sprinkling system, and she'd have to dig to find out. Perhaps order the pipes and fittings she needed, if they weren't the same kind Rogers kept in stock, and get that excavator again. Instead of feeling overwhelmed at the enormity of this job, Cami smiled at the muck.

She loved driving the excavator, loved making broken things whole again, loved seeing the mess get cleaned up.

Locating the leak shouldn't be too hard on this sloped hill. Because the water ran down from where it originated, the leak most likely sat along the line between wet and dry, depending on how long the pipes had been leaking. No matter what, things would need to dry out a little before she brought in the excavator.

She glanced up toward the sky; no clouds in sight. In this Texas fall heat, getting things dry wouldn't be a problem.

After slopping her way back to the principal, she asked, "Do you know what kind of pipes are down there?"

"No idea." He surveyed the field with distaste. "How long will this take?"

"Well." She exhaled. "Things will need to dry out a little bit, and I'll need to dig down to the pipes and find the broken ones. See if we have those in stock. If not, I'll have to order them, and then we'll get it all fixed."

"So nothing today." He wasn't really asking, and he still wouldn't look at her.

"I can come back tonight after my other jobs and check things out." She stared at him, making her gaze as heavy as possible.

"Oh, there's the restoration company from Amarillo. Excuse me." The principal walked away, leaving Cami fuming. She stomped back to Penny and bent to take off her muddy boots.

"I know," she finally said to the van. "He probably just has a lot on his mind. School's in session, and it's football season, and his gym and training room are full of water." She sighed as her anger left her, as she tried to find a reason other than her gender for the dismissive attitude of the principal.

At least she'd be on time for her other two jobs *and* her meeting now. "Let's go, Penny," she said to the van as she twisted the key in the ignition. Penny's engine sputtered to life, and Cami patted the dashboard. "Good girl."

Her next job took longer than expected thanks to a stubborn cold water shut-off valve, and Cami was fifteen minutes late arriving at Rivers Merge for her meeting.

She was just about to get out of her van when a man exited the construction trailer. A man she knew very well and had seen way too often in the past week.

"Wade," she whispered, pressing back into the seat and pulling the door closed again. What was he doing here now? He'd lost the bid. He'd lost the bid to *her*.

Hadn't he?

He carried a folder under his arm, and he moved with confidence the way he always did. This wasn't the countenance she'd seen last week as he'd slunk away with all the other bid-losers while she'd got to go into the trailer and drink that strange sweet tea.

Though she was already late, she waited until he'd gotten in his crisp, white van and driven away before she grabbed her specs and got out of Penny. She kept a prayer going as she mounted the steps and entered the trailer. Nothing seemed off with Gerald, who welcomed her and offered her a plate of hatch chili pepper bread, which she declined. She liked hatch peppers as much as the next Texan, but her insides were already on fire without the aid of the bread.

"So I see some foundations marked," she said, putting the specs she had memorized on the desk between them. "It looks like the foundational plumbing, sewers, and water taps will go in on phase one by the end of the month."

Gerald nodded, a look of mild respect on his face. "Plumbing work should start next Monday."

Relief swept through Cami. She could get the sprinklers at the high school fixed and be ready for the new build. "Sounds great."

"So let's go over the materials," Gerald said.

Cami pulled out a pen and her notebook, all thoughts of Wade Wadsworth fading as she focused on the job. At least that had remained the same in her life, because when she finished the first thing she wanted to do was call Dylan. Share her day with him. Share her life with him.

The thought was as terrifying as it was liberating.

She didn't call him quite yet, but went back to the shop to drop off the specs and put in her invoices and payments from that morning's jobs. Dana sat at the counter, bent over some paperwork.

"Stuff from today," Cami said, laying the checks on the counter with their invoices. She started to go past Dana to put the specs in the cabinet. Otherwise, she'd obsess over them all evening, and she didn't want to do that.

"Camila," Dana said, and Cami turned back to her. "You like working here, right?"

Surprise started in her toes. "Of course I like working here." She didn't just like it, she loved her job with Rogers Plumbing.

"Abraham wants to retire." Dana took off her glasses, her eyes already watering. Cami's chest pinched. They were going to sell the shop. She'd probably need to find another job. Move on. Leave Three Rivers.

The very idea made her suck in a breath and hold it, as the exhalation would be too devastating.

"None of our daughters or their husbands want the shop," Dana said, her voice steady and strong.

Cami's head swam. She needed to breathe. Now. But she didn't know how. Thankfully, her body took over and did the involuntary thing it knew how to do.

She shouldn't have waited for the right time to talk to them about taking over the shop. When was "the right time" anyway?

"Abraham and I would like to offer the shop to you." Dana stood from the stool where she sat. "He's drawn up some preliminary papers for you to look at." She extended a manila folder toward her. "To help you make your decision."

Numbly, Cami reached out and took the folder. The paper felt dry and scratchy against her fingers, and though there were probably only a dozen sheets, it felt like it weighed fifty pounds.

"Are you okay?" Dana asked.

"I thought you were going to tell me I'd need to find a new job." Cami gave a nervous chuckle. "This is so much better. I can't wait to look at it." Giddiness replaced her earlier fear and now she really couldn't wait to talk to Dylan.

∼

HALF AN HOUR LATER, SHE CLIMBED THE STEPS IN DYLAN'S building, having called him to get the address. He'd asked what she was so excited about, but she wanted to tell him in person.

Confusion hit her with every step she took. She'd never wanted to share news with someone in person. "You've never had any news," she muttered to herself. But she hadn't called her parents. She'd called Dylan. She wanted to share things with *him*.

Everything felt new, and strange, and she didn't know what it all meant. Pastor Scott's sermon from yesterday filtered through her mind. Maybe she just needed to trust in the Lord, let Him guide her where she was supposed to go.

She reached the sixth floor where Dylan lived and took a deep breath to calm her racing heart. "Am I supposed to be here?" she wondered aloud, hoping the Lord would tell her to leave if she wasn't.

Instead, a calm, peaceful feeling sank through her, eliminating her worries. She moved down to his door and knocked, the folder clutched tightly in both hands.

He pulled open the door and she drank in the tall sight of him. That handsome face, now brimming with a smile. Those delicious eyes scanning her too. He seemed so happy to see her, and Cami had never felt as safe with someone as she did with Dylan Walker.

She thrust the folder toward him. "Dana and Abraham offered Rogers Plumbing to me. They want to retire."

He stared at the folder with wide eyes and then looked back to her. "Are you serious?"

She shrieked and leapt into his arms. He laughed as he caught her around the waist and twirled her into his apartment. "That's so exciting, Cami."

Every cell in her body felt like it was having a birthday party. She exhaled and found her footing, noticing that Dylan didn't step back or remove his hands from her hips. She glanced up, right into his face, and found him gazing at her, a look of pure adoration in those ocean-turquoise eyes.

The moment lengthened; that something sparked; Cami tipped up onto her toes to kiss him even though she hadn't gone home to shower first, even though her stomach roared for something to eat, even though her previous fears about moving too fast with Dylan had returned and were screaming through her skull.

Kissing Dylan quieted everything, forced it all outside of her immediate presence. His hands cradled her face, holding her in place as he smoothed her hair back. "I'm so happy for you." He touched his mouth to her cheek, her temple, along her ear. "Have you looked at the offer yet?"

"I glanced at it," she said breathlessly as his lips trailed down her throat. "You said something about having dinner?"

"Mm," he said, the sound originating in his throat and not making it much farther. He made no move to go into the kitchen, no indication that he'd be doing anything but kissing her tonight.

And honestly, that was just fine with Cami. She laid the folder on the back of his couch and put both arms around him, holding onto him as he continued to kiss her, sending shockwaves of butterflies to every extremity in her body.

He pulled back gently and held her against his chest. "I've got hot egg and cheese sandwiches in the oven."

The scent of the food met her nose, and Cami was surprised she hadn't smelled it earlier. In her excitement over the offer and her extreme focus on Dylan, she supposed she'd missed a lot of things.

"Sounds great," she said, stepping back and reaching for her folder. "Let's look at this while we eat."

Dylan ducked around her, a flush in his face that Cami found adorable. He pulled the food out of the oven and put it on two plates while she sat at his table-for-two barely outside of the kitchen.

She placed one palm on the folder. "Do you think I can qualify for a loan for the business?"

"Of course. The Three Rivers Bank gives special rates to locals." He put a sandwich cut on the diagonal in front of her. She didn't know how to make it fit with what she knew about Dylan.

"And besides, you live right next door to the guy who gives out the loans." He shrugged. "Seemed like you and Carole Anne were pretty close." He watched her, and Cami's face heated.

"So I told her about you," she said, thinking of her punishing kick-boxing session from that morning. "And she challenged me to call you. That was all."

"But you didn't."

"Actually, I did."

He peered at her, those eyes watching her with extreme interest. So much so that he ignored his food. "I did not get a call from you."

"The call just didn't connect before I freaked out and hung up." She stared at him for another moment and then laughed. "Besides, you used the after-hours emergency line to call me."

"And it worked."

She rolled her eyes and picked up her sandwich to take a bite. After chewing and swallowing, she said, "So I'll go talk to Levi tomorrow."

Dylan took a long drink of his water. "What time are you gonna go? Maybe I could come with you."

Cami's chest cinched, and she took another bite of her sandwich. "If you want."

Dylan watched her for a moment past comfortable, then dropped his gaze to his plate and set down his sandwich. "So you don't want me to." He wasn't asking.

Cami didn't know what to say, didn't know why she didn't want him to come. *Yes, you do*, a voice whispered in her head. *Be honest and tell him.*

She took a breath and prepared to speak.

CHAPTER THIRTEEN

Dylan didn't hear much past, "Dylan, I'm scared." Cami kept talking, but Dylan could only solve one problem at a time.

A few more words obviously entered his mind, because when she finished, he said, "Cami, we can go as slow as you want."

"It's just that I have a lot going on right now, especially with the new build, and the high school gym is full of water, and now I have to figure out financing...."

"Pipes at the high school?" Dylan felt like he could eat again, so he picked up his sandwich and took another bite. Cami told him about the leak there, the flooded gym, the meeting with Gerald, all of it.

Dylan liked listening to her talk. Liked that she'd come over after work. Liked not being alone and not relying on Boone for company.

So even though he'd just said they could go slow, nothing

in his thought pattern was going less than sixty miles per hour.

They finished eating and moved to the couch, where she showed him the offer. It looked good—a reasonable amount of money for the shop, the building, all the equipment, the insurance, the van.

"It's everything you want," he said, glad she'd leaned back into his chest a while ago.

"It is." She finally closed the folder and relaxed, and Dylan definitely thought he could get used to having her in his life like this. But he switched on the TV and let it carry them through the next bout of silence.

When she left, Dylan kissed her carefully but not deeply, and she was the one to take them to the next level. Dylan stopped it almost immediately, ducking his head and licking his lips to taste her again. "You should go." He lifted his gaze to her, his meaning clear. *Can't stay and kiss me like that and expect me to go slow.*

"Yeah, sure. See you later." She pressed the folder to her chest and went down the hall, a smile on her face.

Dylan closed the door and leaned into it, a sigh hissing out of his chest like a leaky balloon. "You're in too deep," he told himself as he moved their plates from the table to the sink. But he didn't know how to get out. Wasn't even sure he wanted to. And that was a whole new feeling for him that he'd have to figure out.

∽

LATER THAT WEEK, HE REALLY WANTED TO SEE CAMI

again, but his "slow game" plan was to wait at least three days before contacting her. Now, if she called or texted him before the seventy-two-hours ended, great. But he wasn't going to pressure her to see him.

She really did have a lot going on, as all the foundational plumbing at the build needed to be done and he didn't have much business up there for a while.

So he focused on the upcoming Christmas parade, and he scheduled a few hours every morning to go over to the city storage units to check out the vehicles that had been moved there.

When he arrived on Friday morning after a fun evening with the veterans at Courage Reins, he whistled as he entered the huge warehouse.

As Halloween approached, the air cooled a bit, especially in the morning and evenings, and the warehouse wasn't too hot yet.

He picked up the clipboard that hung on a nail next to the door and scanned the list of vehicles the city would be using in this year's parade. There were thirteen this year, and Dylan sighed as he saw the Elf Tree House and Santa's Workshop.

Those floats had dozens of moving parts, and they never worked from year to year. Sometimes he had to rewire the entire float to get all the elves to rotate, and one year he went through the lightbulbs one by one on the workshop float in order to make sure everything that was supposed to flash, in fact, flashed.

He glanced up from the clipboard, a sigh passing through

his body. "Not starting with either of those," he said, walking past the tree house with a pointed glare.

Instead, he stopped next to the Reindeer Galore float and started by checking the electronics panel. All the cords looked good, like they could easily be plugged into the aux inputs of a car.

He got to work, checking all the wires, the connections, and finally climbing up and then down into the car. After hooking everything up, he started the vehicle and said a little prayer.

He got back up onto the float and walked around the reindeer, checking for the lights and motion that should be working now that the electricity was flowing.

This float had never given him much trouble, and it didn't today either. He flipped pages until he found the Reindeer Galore sheet and he began checking boxes.

Dasher, Dancer, Prancer, Vixen.... One by one, he went through each reindeer and made sure everything that needed to be checked was checked. Even Rudolph's nose didn't give him any trouble, and Dylan moved onto the next vehicle.

He didn't quite make it through all the checks on the Three Little Snowmen float before it was time for him to get back to the office, but there was still plenty of time before the parade to get everything up and running.

He texted Bill on his way out, letting him know what he'd done and that he'd recorded it all on the clipboard.

Thanks, Bill sent back. I'll try to be there next week.

It wasn't necessary, and sometimes Bill slowed Dylan down, but if he wanted to come over and watch Dylan check wires, he wasn't going to tell him no.

Back at the office, he checked his phone, hoping Cami had texted him during the short drive between the warehouse and the Electric Company.

Her texts during their three-day hiatuses became less frequent as she struggled to keep up with everything going on in her life. Dylan knew she was stressed with getting all the paperwork started for the loan to buy the plumbing shop, knew the high school job had set her behind in her regular work, knew she was working twelve hours a day just to keep up and not lose any customers. After all, the build would last for two years, but she'd need the support of the community long after that.

Still, he missed her. He wanted to see her every night, not every third. He wanted to hold her, and kiss her, and confide in her in person, not through a text. He hadn't felt like this about a woman before, and he didn't know what to do.

So he didn't invite himself to her Friday night horseback riding sessions, and he didn't complain when he didn't get to see her on Saturday.

He'd invited her to church, and she'd said she'd sit by him and they could go back to her place afterward, something they'd been doing for the past couple of weeks. She had a swing on her back deck, and it was peaceful and quiet there, and he could kiss her whenever he wanted.

And he and Cami would see each other two days in a row, because the barbecue at his parent's place was on Monday night. "You're still good for the barbecue tomorrow, right?" he asked as he and Cami left church together. He didn't want to appear desperate, but he couldn't imagine having to show up by himself.

"Yeah, I think so."

She thought so? He quirked an eyebrow at her, but she didn't see it as she focused on the railroad tracks across the street.

"I have a couple of jobs I said I'd catch up on in the morning." She danced in front of him and smiled. "But I should be good by three."

"Great, I'll come pick you up a few minutes before that." He beamed down at her but kept his hands in his pockets.

Her golden eyes sparkled like diamonds, and Dylan's thoughts soared to the gem. He'd been thinking about them a lot lately, which was ridiculous. He and Cami had been dating for a month, and she'd expressly said she thought things were moving too fast.

That was weeks ago, he told himself.

"Let's go for a drive today," Cami said as he extracted his keys and unlocked his truck.

"Where do you want to go?"

"Let's explore a little. Do you know the area very well?"

"Sure, I grew up here."

"Take me somewhere amazing then." She gave him one of her gorgeous, full smiles.

"Can we eat first?"

She laughed, tossing her hair over her shoulder. "Eating is a given. But maybe we can find somewhere we've never been."

Dylan's stomach growled, but he told it to behave. "I like this adventurous side of you." He slid her a sideways glance. "She doesn't come out much, does she?"

"She's hidden behind the seriousness of paying bills and

fixing pipes," Cami admitted. She slid across the seat and lifted the console so she could sit right by him.

"Is this your adventurous side too?" He took her hand in his. "Because now I really like her."

She giggled and said, "No, this is the side of me that really likes you."

Dylan forced himself to coast to a stop at the sign. He looked down at her. "I really like you too, Camila." He leaned over and kissed her. This kiss could've really morphed into something serious, something full and round that he'd never forget, something new between them starting after only a few seconds.

But someone behind him honked, startling him away from Cami and eliciting another giggle from her.

"We'll get back to that," he said gruffly as he eased through the intersection and set the truck on the road leading past Rivers Merge and north out of town. "Have you ever been up to the Oklahoma border?" he asked.

"Nope. Is there something exciting out there?"

"I don't know if I'd label it as exciting," he said. "But just across the border, there's this tiny little town. I used to go up there with my friends. They serve two things: meat and frozen yogurt."

Cami scoffed. "Those two things don't really seem like they go together."

"They really do, though." He felt the weight of her gaze on the side of his face, and he glanced at her. "What? They do."

"So you dip your ribs in yogurt."

"No, ew." He laughed. "But the ribs are savory and delicious, and I won't lie, I've dipped my French fries in the yogurt. It's good." A few seconds passed before he remembered something else. "Oh, and they're only open until Halloween, so today's a great day to go. They'll close tomorrow."

"I hope the winter slows down a little," she said, sighing. "But I don't see that happening. Rivers Merge is a two-year project."

Dylan didn't want to talk about work, so he just said, "Yep," and asked her if she'd been to the three rivers that had given the town its name.

"Once, when I was little," she said.

"Well, let's go there," he said.

"We don't have our swimming suits. We're still in our church clothes."

He looked at her, his pulse spiking at the mere sight of her. He hoped it always would. "That's the adventure, sweetheart."

~

Dylan felt like someone had taken out his heart and grilled it before stuffing it back inside his chest. He couldn't stop thinking about grilling, and potato salad, and watermelon. All things his mom had planned or made for the barbecue he and Cami had just arrived for.

"You ready?" he asked from the safety of his truck.

"You know, I think I am." Cami smiled at him and opened the door to get out, a picture of ease, but Dylan knew she had no idea what she was getting into. His older sisters had always been more like mothers to him than sisters, and Second-Mom wasn't better than Third- or Fourth-Mom.

But he got out of the truck too, following Cami up the sidewalk to his parents' front porch. She wore a sleeveless shirt the color of apricots and a pair of black jeans. Her lean legs extended down to a pair of simple sandals with more buckles than Dylan knew shoes could have. She'd added a curl to her hair and extra eye makeup to her face today, all of which Dylan liked.

In fact, he was having a hard time disliking anything about her, and he felt himself getting close to the Dangerous Line again. The one that urged him to stomp on the accelerator and make a trip to the jeweler in Amarillo.

He slipped his hand into hers as he stepped past her to open the door. "They'll be out back," he said, sure his mom would have the spread already on the tables in anticipation of meeting Cami.

He caught Alecia moving through the sliding glass door, saying, "Get that last bowl, Ruthie. They'll be here any minute."

His oldest niece, Ruthie, picked up a green bowl of salad a moment before she saw Dylan. "Uncle Dylan!" She almost dropped the bowl back onto the counter before rushing toward him.

He released Cami's hand to receive his niece. "Hey-ya, Ruthie. How've you been?"

She giggled in his arms and said, "Mama's teachin' me the piano now."

"Oh yeah?" He thought of his oldest sister and her

unyielding rules for chores and meal times. He imagined what a piano lesson with her would be like and his appreciation for his niece grew.

"Yeah, I can play a couple of songs. Wanna hear?"

"I'm sure—"

"After lunch, Ruthie." Alecia filled the doorway leading outside, her words of the no-nonsense variety. She tucked her blonde hair behind her ear and smiled at Cami. "You must be Camila." She came forward and hugged Cami, who didn't seem uncomfortable with the hello whatsoever.

"And you must be Alecia." Cami stepped back and smiled at her. "And you're Ruthie, obviously."

Dylan put Ruthie down, and Alecia pointed to the salad bowl. "Mom's got everything set up outside." She followed Ruthie outside with the salad, and Dylan took a deep breath.

"That wasn't so bad," Cami said.

"That's the tip of the iceberg," he muttered, stepping through the sliding glass door first.

CHAPTER FOURTEEN

Cami felt like she'd been thrown into a fast food restaurant play place. Kids seemed to be *every*where, and they all dropped what they were doing to swarm toward Dylan. Choruses of "Uncle Dylan!" and "Uncle Dylan's here!" rang through the sky, almost deafening Cami.

She got the heck out of the way before she got trampled by a dozen under-ten-year-olds. Dylan got mobbed, but his bass laughter could be heard above the higher shrills of his nieces and nephews.

"He's obviously well-liked," a woman said. Not Alecia. She grinned at her younger brother. "I'm Sally, the middle sister."

"Cami."

Sally was also a hugger, which didn't bother Cami as much as it normally did. Maybe the bear hug from Sister One had prepped her for all the hugging. Because Dylan's mom came next, and she had the shine of tears in her eyes.

Cami was very curious about what Dylan had told them about her, but she kept her smile in place and allowed the hugging.

Rose, the youngest, giggled during the hug, sobering long enough to say, "He really likes you, you know." She held onto Cami's shoulders for an extra moment and stepped back, only to be replaced by Dylan's tall, tanned father.

Who also hugged her.

Cami was hugged out for the year by the time Dylan unburied himself from the small humans and his dad retreated back to the grill. Dylan returned to her, several of the kids coming with him.

"You okay?" he asked, taking one look at her and wrapping one arm around her shoulders.

"Fine." But she leaned into his strength, taking it for herself.

"Guys," Dylan said to his nieces and nephews. "This is Cami." He squeezed her shoulder, and she waved to the kids.

"Hey, guys." She grinned. These Walker's made cute kids, with blonde hair and blue eyes for miles. "Tell me your names."

"Start down there," Dylan drawled in his Texan tone. He pointed to the left end of the row.

"Michael," the boy said.

"Taryn."

"Lisa."

"Bryant."

"Boyd." He was clearly the youngest, but had the oldest name, and Cami's heart softened toward the cute boy.

"Nice to meet you all."

"Go on, now," Dylan said. "We'll come play in a few minutes."

The kids scattered, leaving Cami holding onto Dylan. "We will?" she asked.

"*I* will," he amended.

"And you'll leave me at the adult table, is that it?"

He looked down at her, surprise in his eyes which softened into cute little crinkles as he chuckled. "I guess I won't need to escape the adult table today."

"You normally do?"

"Dylan!" his mother called. "Come on, baby. We're ready to eat."

"Baby?" Cami stifled a laugh.

"She calls everyone baby or honey," he said, an anxious look crossing his face as he surveyed the backyard. "This is insane, right?"

"I like them," Cami said. Her heart warmed at the double-long picnic table his parents had obviously had special-made for this exact occasion. Moms and dads helped kids get quiet, and Dylan's dad turned from the grill.

"Are we ready?" he asked.

"Sh," Dylan's mom said to Boyd, and then she said, "Let's pray, guys. Get ready."

"Sally, will you say it?" their dad asked, and Sally nodded.

Cami bowed her head and folded her arms like everyone else. Immediately, a sense of peace descended on the backyard, penetrating her heart and making tears heat the back of her eyelids.

She hadn't felt this accepted, this loved, in a long time. Her parents were fine; they were. But they didn't have

Sunday meals together, or family barbecues. Her older brother worked non-stop, and Cami did too.

She'd thought that was all she needed.

She'd been wrong.

Once the prayer ended, the chaos started again. But Cami didn't mind. This activity, this energy, was better than the staleness that had infected her life. She left Dylan's side and joined the line behind one of the husbands.

"You look familiar," she said, hoping that was an appropriate way to start a conversation.

"You came and fixed our garbage disposal last year."

"Oh, right." Cami smiled and asked Dylan's dad for one of the vegetable skewers. He gave her a skeptical look but found the shish-kabob without any meat on it and gave it to her.

"There's three for her." Dylan's mom came bustling over. "Dylan told us all about how you're a vegetarian. There's watermelon, and potato salad, and macaroni, and Emmy and I made three veggie-kabobs for you."

"Thank you, ma'am." Cami nodded. "I'll be fine."

"Give her another one, Troy." She swatted her husband's forearm.

"Ma," Dylan said. "Leave her alone."

"I just want to make sure she gets enough to eat."

Oh, Cami would get enough to eat. That was a guarantee. If not here, then at home. Or a drive-through. "Thanks," she said. "I'm okay, really."

Dylan's mom wore a look that said she wasn't sure, but she didn't say anything. Dylan got two hamburgers and then loaded his plate with potato chips and watermelon before turning back to the picnic table.

"Looks like they left us a spot right in the middle," he grumbled. "I'm so sorry about this, Cami." He had a panicked look in his eye. "I feel like I should've warned you better."

"You warned me fine." Cami eyed the narrow gap between his oldest sister and his youngest. "I'm fine, Dylan. Really."

But if she had to tell one more person that, she might not be fine.

~

A WEEK LATER, CAMI WAS STILL THINKING ABOUT THE barbecue. She'd enjoyed herself. Really enjoyed herself. They'd talked and she'd answered questions. No one said the word *girlfriend*, and they'd played horseshoes and then badminton.

It had been a perfect afternoon in Texas.

Which this afternoon definitely was not.

She'd been waiting at the bank for a half an hour. A half an hour she didn't have to be wasted doing nothing. She had invoices to file, and phone calls to return, and supplies to order for the next stage of the build at Rivers Merge.

But she wanted the Rogers's plumbing shop, and so she waited. She'd gotten very good at waiting over the past few weeks. Three days before seeing Dylan. Three days before he'd ask her to come over.

She was tired of it, and she'd seen him every day last week after the barbecue. And it felt good, right.

"Cami?"

She glanced up to see Levi. "Come on back." He wore a happy smile on his face, and Cami hoped he had the news she wanted.

Cami stood, taking an extra moment to balance in her heels. "Thank you." She followed him down a short hallway and away from the normal business of the bank. He entered a room, which held an impressive office with a towering desk filling almost all of it.

They shook hands, and Cami set her folder on the desk as she perched in the available chair.

"Thanks for coming in," he said. "I know it can be a bit of a hassle." He kept the smile in place. "Carole Anne's been on me to get you in here for a week.

Cami nodded and tried to keep her smile normal, not wanting to give away that she'd rescheduled two jobs to be here this afternoon.

"So I asked to see the profit and loss statements for the plumbing business."

"Yes." Cami straightened and opened her folder. "I have them for the past five years, and you can see...." She slid a paper across the table. "The shop is doing well enough. Some months are leaner than others, but there's a nice profit at the end of each year."

She wasn't sure what the profit and loss statements would affect. He'd already assured her that yes, she'd get the special local rate, and he'd said her financials were all in order. He peered at the papers Dana had provided for an agonizingly long time.

"And you'll run the shop alone?" He glanced up.

"Yes, sir," she said, her annoyance already climbing.

He glanced up. "And you and Dylan...you're not engaged or anything."

"My boyfriend works for the city, but no. He's an electrician, not a plumber." She tacked a laugh onto the end of the statement as she realized what she'd just said.

My boyfriend.

"He's a good man. Grew up with his sisters."

Cami nodded, unsure of how to contribute. Dylan was a good man. She'd never seen him miss church. He adored his nieces and nephews, and they adored him. He helped out his family, visited them, was involved in their lives.

And she'd called him her boyfriend. She wished she'd told him first that she'd thought of him like that, and she hoped Levi wouldn't say anything to him.

"Thanks for bringing these in," he said. "We just want to make sure you'll be able to make the payments on the loan, and all of this looks fantastic." He reached for the folder and pulled it toward him. "I'll put them in your file."

"Thank you." Cami stood, her mind racing. She let herself out and practically ran to Penny. "I called him my boyfriend," she told the van. "What should I do?"

Penny didn't answer, but she did seem to be pulling to the north, toward Dylan's building. So Cami made the required turns, hoping it was God and not some defunct van that was leading her to Dylan.

CHAPTER FIFTEEN

*D*ylan didn't see Cami's calls until he left Rivers Merge. They were putting up houses like lightning, and he'd just met with Gerald to schedule the first rough electrical work on the first six houses, all of which were framed and getting their roofs this week.

He'd forgotten how quickly homes went up once the financing came through and all the tradesmen were hired. It had been a while since Three Rivers had seen a build the size of Rivers Merge.

He hit call to dial Cami back, and said, "Hey, sweetheart," when she picked up.

"Where are you?" she asked.

"Just left Rivers Merge. Where you at?"

"Your place."

Surprise mingled with pleasure. "Oh yeah?" he asked, though they'd been getting together every night after work for the past week. He liked that a whole lot better than the three-day dance they'd been doing previously. Liked having her beside him. Liked kissing her goodnight.

"Yeah, I have to tell you something."

"I'll be there in five." He threw his notes on the passenger side of the seat. "Unless you just want to tell me now."

"I—you didn't say you grew up with Levi."

"I grew up with everyone who still lives here."

"Are you friends with any of them still?"

"I mean, I'd say hello if I saw them, but I can't say we hang out or anything, especially Levi. He's more Alecia's age than mine."

She exhaled. "I called you my boyfriend when I was at the bank today."

Dylan's muscles froze for three terrifying heartbeats as he drove without really directing the truck. Then he started laughing.

"What?" she asked. "Stop it." But she started giggling too.

"That's great," he said. "So can I call you my girlfriend? My mom's been askin' about you."

"I think you could call me that, yes."

He turned onto his street, glad he could navigate himself again. "Will you say it?"

"What do you mean?"

"I want to hear you say you're my girlfriend."

"Dylan."

"Camila." He pulled into his assigned parking spot and left his notes right where they were.

"I'm your girlfriend. Happy now?"

"Not when you say it like that." He laughed as he got out of his truck. "I think you should have to shout it from my window. Then everyone will know."

She scoffed. "Like they don't already."

"You think they do?"

"We go to church together every week. You're always holding my hand when we leave."

"You like that," he said, almost a question. He couldn't tell if she was upset or her tone had just turned a little frosty for some other reason.

"Sure, yeah, of course I do."

"You don't?"

"Dylan." Her voice hit his ears in two different ways. Over the phone and very nearby. She came around the corner wearing a skirt and heels and completely taking him by surprise. She lowered her phone and smiled the sexiest smile Dylan had ever seen. "I like holding your hand."

He ended the call and chuckled. "You know I have nothing to eat, right?"

"We can order something."

"Chinese?" He approached and took her in his arms. He sighed, everything relaxed and happy to have Cami so close.

"Chinese it is."

"Why you all dressed up?" he asked as they headed toward the elevator.

"I had a meeting at the bank."

"Oh, right. Where you told Levi Thomlinson I was your *boyfriend*." He danced away as she tried to slap his bicep.

"You're impossible." The elevator arrived and she stalked

onto it. Well, in her heels she couldn't really stalk, so she sort of sashayed.

He followed her. "And you're stunning in that skirt, those heels." He whistled as he drank her in, heels to eyes. The elevator doors closed behind him. "I'm going to kiss you now." He leaned down, glad when she fisted her fingers in the collar of his Electric Company shirt and brought him toward her.

Every kiss felt like the first one, and Dylan would've kept going if not for the alarming chime that they'd arrived on the sixth floor.

Thanksgiving approached, and Dylan couldn't remember when he'd been so busy. If he wasn't at the build site, he was prepping to go. Ordering supplies, reading up on installing hot water heaters, or packing trucks with wires and outlet boxes. If he wasn't doing that, he was thinking about the homes at Rivers Merge. Twin homes took up the back and would be built in stage four. The condos would take up stage three. Single family homes dominated stages one and two, and last he'd heard, they were selling fast.

Should he get one?

He couldn't stop thinking about it, and that usually meant he needed to do something. He'd tried praying, but no answer had come. It was almost as if God didn't care where he lived.

He and Cami still managed to see each other, sometimes out at Rivers Merge if they were lucky. He spent his evenings with her, and he learned everything about her, from how she took her coffee to why she couldn't go back to Amarillo.

One night, with only a couple of weeks until the first night of the Christmas parade, Cami entered the warehouse where he'd finally decided to tackle the Elf Tree House, carrying a couple of bags of fast food.

"Burgers," she said. "And I stopped by the bakery. Grace was just closing up, so she gave me everything at half price." Cami wore a satisfied smile, like she'd been given something special. Dylan wasn't sure how often she went to the bakery, but they always sold everything for fifty percent off in the last thirty minutes before they closed.

"Thanks," he said, taking a bag of food and sweeping a kiss across her mouth. "How was work?"

"Oh, you know. Only one toilet to service today." She sighed as she climbed onto the sleigh and pulled out an apple fritter. She grinned just before taking a bite of it.

Dylan smiled and shook his head before focusing on the elves again. There were just so many of them. Did Santa really need that much help to get everything ready for Christmas?

He reminded himself that his mother put together an entire binder for a barbecue, so yes, Santa probably needed the dozens of elves in order to pull off Christmas.

Thankfully, this float only had sixteen elves—and at the moment, ten of them were working. He started working on the bearded one, deciding to reward himself with his food if he got the elf to turn its head the way it was supposed to.

Fifteen minutes later, Cami had finished all of her sweets, and he finally got the elf to move.

"A-ha!" he said triumphantly. And the blue light on the

elf's hat lit up too. He grabbed the food bag and climbed into the sleigh with Cami.

She grinned at him and he reached into the bag and handed her a box of French fries. "We're going to the parade together, right?" he asked.

"It runs for weeks," she said. "Which one do you want to go to?"

"The first one." He glanced at her as he unwrapped his cheeseburger. "First weekend in December. Friday night."

"Yeah, sure." She leaned back against the seat and closed her eyes. She was positively angelic, and Dylan wondered if she was too tired for serious conversation.

She did work more than anyone should have to, but he knew he would do the same for a better future.

"Hey," he said gently when he'd eaten through his burger. "I was wondering...how you felt about children."

Her eyes jerked open, a familiar edge of fear there. "Children?"

"Yeah, do you, uh, you know, want kids?"

She sat up, her eyes never leaving his. "Um—"

"In general," he said. "Do you see yourself having a family someday?"

"Someday," she repeated slowly. "Yeah, sure." She looked out of the sleigh at something that wasn't there in warehouse.

"How many?" He popped a few fries in his mouth.

She glanced at him, a knowing light in her eyes. "One or two."

He scoffed. "That's ridiculous." He grinned at her so

she'd know he was kidding. "I want a whole houseful of them."

"Well, how big is the house you're getting?"

He fell silent. "Well, I was thinking about getting one up in the new development. But I don't know." He didn't want to put in a yard or deal with no shade. He liked the older parts of Three Rivers better, but he'd done nothing to look at the real estate market.

"So for my house, one or two is a houseful." She ate a few more fries. "I don't know. I just don't see myself as very nurturing. Or something."

"You're nurturing," he said. "You were great with my nieces and nephews."

"I guess."

He lifted his arm and she cuddled into his side, and while they were sitting in a fake sleigh in a warehouse in a state where it rarely snowed, Dylan felt like he was about to have the best Christmas of his life.

∽

A WEEK LATER, ON BLACK FRIDAY, DYLAN STARTED looking for diamonds. He got up early and drove to the only jeweler in town, hoping he wouldn't have to go all the way to Amarillo. He had no plans to work or see Camila for the rest of the day. He hoped one of those would change, but for now, he didn't want her to know where he was or what he was doing.

The sky threatened rain as Dylan found himself in the

jewelry store in Amarillo. It hadn't been hard to go inside. Or to tell the salesman why he was there.

But the selection of diamonds—from cut to color to quality—was daunting, to say the least. Boone had offered to come with him, but Dylan had turned him down. For some reason, he wanted this experience to be his, and his alone.

"What about this one?" Roman, the salesman, held up a ring nestled in a box, the baseball-diamond shaped gem, and Dylan's heart went pitter-pat. "This is our popular princess cut but set sideways."

"I like that," Dylan said. The band was silver and thin and didn't seem strong enough to support such a huge diamond.

"It has a second piece," Roman said, plucking another ring from the counter in front of him. Dylan knew him from around town, as Roman had grown up in Three Rivers and followed his father into the diamond business. He was several years older than Dylan though, closer to Alecia's age.

"You keep this piece until the wedding day, and your bride-to-be wears the diamond. Then, once you're married, you unite the two pieces. She could have it soldered then, to keep the ring together."

Roman slipped the diamond out of the box and put the two rings together. The thicker silver second piece definitely gave the ring a whole new look—one Dylan really liked.

Swallowing, he glanced down the case of rings, no idea what he was looking for. Oh, yes, he did. A price tag. Some indication of how much this was going to cost.

"This one is affordable," Roman said, as if sensing Dylan's hesitation.

"Oh yeah?" Dylan drawled. "Define 'affordable'."

"You work for the city, right?"

Dylan cocked his head. "Yeah."

"I think you came out last fall when my furnace was on the fritz."

"Sounds like something a heating and air conditioning company would do," Dylan said. "I work with the Electric Company."

"No, it was you. The power to the entire unit was down. You fixed it." Roman beamed at him like Dylan had accomplished world peace.

"All right," Dylan said. "How much?"

"This ring is normally thirty-five hundred dollars—"

Dylan sputtered and choked, heat rushing to his face.

"But," Roman said quickly. "It's seventy percent off for our holiday sale. That makes it...." He pulled a handheld calculator toward him and started beating on the buttons to calculate the price.

"One thousand fifty dollars," Roman concluded. "And I can give you an addition ten percent for being a city employee, which makes it—" *Tap, tap, tap, punch.*

"Nine hundred forty-five dollars."

"And tax," Dylan said. Which would be the ten percent back on.

"Plus tax." Roman started typing again, and Dylan picked up the ring. He liked it a whole lot, just like he liked Cami a whole lot.

He shook his head. He wasn't buying a diamond ring for a woman he liked a whole lot.

He was buying a diamond ring for the woman he loved.

"I'll take it," Dylan said, placing it delicately back in the silk of the box. He simultaneously felt like throwing up and throwing a party.

Now all he needed to do was figure out if Cami would say yes when he asked her to marry him, and at the moment, his gut was telling him that if he showed up with a diamond, she'd freak out and retreat.

But that was okay. He tucked the bag with the ring in it into his glove box. He could wait.

CHAPTER SIXTEEN

Cami drove past two Christmas tree stalls on the way to Rivers Merge. An idea occurred to her that she should get a tree on the way home and get her place ready for the holidays. She usually put her tree up the day after Thanksgiving, and she shouldn't even be working today. But she had a lot of work to do, and there wouldn't be anyone else at the site today.

She thought through the tradition she'd established for herself after she moved out of her parent's house when she was only nineteen. Gold and red balls. White lights. A real tree so the air became scented with pine. And she decided she'd definitely get a tree on the way home and then dig through her attic until she found her Christmas decor.

She pulled into the construction parking lot behind the trailer and exhaled as she got out of Penny-the-Plumbing-Van.

"See you later, girl." Cami tapped the window of the van

and headed around the trailer to get the reports on the phase one homes. She'd been at the build site every day, six days a week, for the past six weeks, doing the rough plumbing home by home, with the roofers following behind her, and Dylan coming in right after them to do his wiring.

After she got all the bones in place, she didn't have to come back to the home until the finishing work needed to be completed. Then she and Dylan would switch positions, and he'd go through the home before, doing the finishing electrical work like installing switches, doorbells, outlets, and connecting all the appliances to power.

She'd install the sinks, toilets, and faucets and from there, it was mirror work and carpet installation, final clean up, and then families would be living in the shell of a home Cami had put pipes in when it was just a concrete slab.

She still had two homes to get plumbed before next weekend, and she had eight working days to do it. That was an insane amount of work—it usually took her a full week of ten-hour days to get a house plumbed, and the roofing crew had been breathing down her neck since the build began.

Her back and neck already ached at the thought of smashing a twelve-day job into only eight days, but she'd already talked to Gerald about it. He'd said they could roof the last house while she was in it if that would keep everyone on schedule.

She'd agreed, and so had the Snell's, the family owned and operated roofing company that sat on the edge of town, along the highway leading to Amarillo.

As soon as she opened the door to the trailer, she knew something was different. Like a scent on the air, the vibe in the room hit her like a punch. She froze, glancing around the room to take in who was there, and why, and what had happened.

Dylan rose from Gerald's desk, a to-go cup of coffee in his hand. "I knew you'd be in today." He grinned at her and extended the cup toward her though she was several paces away.

"I have two houses to plumb still," she said, knowing he'd slow her down if he stayed. But she didn't want to be rude, and she did love the coffee from the pancake house. So she crossed the trailer and took it from him. "Thanks."

"I'm not staying," he said, getting to his feet. "I did a little shopping this morning, and my mother wants to do family pictures now."

"Sounds fun."

"Oh, it's so not," he said. "My sisters get their kids all worked up before we even get there, and everyone leaves crying. Well, except for me. Last year, even the photographer was crying by the end, but I think that was out of relief that it was over."

Cami laughed. "Family pictures with your crew would be comical." She took a sip of her coffee. "I was just going to log in and get to work."

"What are you doing later?" He stood and took her into his arms, making her feel warm and a smile come to her face.

"I'm going to buy a Christmas tree on the way home. Get it set up." She gazed up at him, wondering if it was time to start a new tradition. "You want to help me?"

He blinked and softness entered those blue eyes. "Yeah," he said slowly. "I'd love that." He leaned down and kissed her, and Cami kept it slow and heated, passionate yet unrushed.

"Mm." He broke their connection and tucked her close to his heartbeat. Cami stayed there, her own pulse rapid firing in a strange, new way. She wondered if she was falling in love with Dylan—or if she was already there.

"So I'll come by later," he said. "I think I'm going to see what's for sale after pictures."

"Houses?"

"Yeah."

"Up here."

He shook his head. "Nah. I'm going to go with something a little bit more...established."

Cami watched him walk out, her heart doing that skipping again.

Later, she told herself. She'd have to figure out how she felt about Dylan later. Right now, she had a lot of plumbing work to do.

Hours later, with aching fingers and loud complaints from her back, she pulled into a Christmas tree lot. There were many more cars here now, especially now that it was almost dark.

She joined the throng of people wandering around looking at trees, thinking she needed to get one she could get into the van by herself. Well, someone would help her get it into the van, but she'd need to get it into her house.

She found a nice seven-foot-tall tree, with little spindly branches at the top. They wouldn't hold a star, but she never put one on her tree anyway.

Sure enough, a teenage worker helped her get the tree

into the van, and she headed home. When she turned the corner onto her street, Dylan's big white truck sat out front, and a huge smile sprang to her face.

So maybe she liked him a whole lot. She still wasn't sure if she was in love with him.

She parked Penny in the driveway and got out, crossing the lawn and meeting Dylan on the sidewalk. "How long have you been here?"

"Twenty minutes or so."

"I don't have any food here." She slipped her arms around his waist and grinned up at him.

"You're here," he said, and somehow those were the two nicest words Cami had ever heard. "We can order something. Did you get a tree?"

"Yeah, Penny's got her." They moved over to the van, where Cami opened both of the back doors to reveal the tree. "Let's get it inside."

Dylan did most of the heavy lifting, but Cami helped a little, especially getting the wider bottom of the tree through the narrow door. She scurried around to move the recliner out of the way and then she pushed the couch down while Dylan balanced the tree in the doorway.

"I want it over here by the fireplace," she said, and he muscled the tree where she wanted it, twisting the screw into the trunk to keep it straight and upright.

She stood by the front door, and he joined her. "Looks great there."

"I have to get up into the attic to get all the ornaments." Her stomach growled and Dylan looked down at it.

"Let's eat first, okay? I don't want you on any ladders until then."

"I could eat," she said. "Pizza?"

"I never say no to pizza."

She pulled out her phone and ordered a meat-lovers pizza, as well as an order of penne pasta and a side salad. After she hung up, she asked, "Did you find any houses?"

"Yeah, you wanna see?"

"Of course." She smiled at him, and he pulled out his phone.

"Okay, I saved a few. My dad says I need a realtor, so I'll probably call one next week." He went out on the front steps and sat on the top one while he swiped and tapped. "I like this one."

She sat next to him and took the phone from him. The first picture showed an older home that looked like it had been recently painted red. The front door was black, and two tall plants stood sentinel on either side.

"That one's three bedrooms," he said. "And it has a shed in the backyard."

"A shed?" She glanced at him. "What do you need a shed for?"

"I don't know," he said. "It sounds very manly."

Cami tipped her head back and laughed. "It looks like it has some good upgrades," she said, swiping to see the new floors in the kitchen and the granite countertops in the bathrooms. "Two bathrooms too."

"Mm hm." He peered over her shoulder. "I liked it. But it's way down on the south edge of town, and there are tons of bugs down there."

"This is Texas," she said, handing the phone back to him. "There are bugs everywhere."

"But more down there," he said, swiping. "They put in that stupid fountain and apparently it attracts a lot of mosquitoes. There's this one too. It's only a couple of blocks from here."

She took the phone from him again, her eyes catching on his for a few extra seconds. The thought of having him only a block or two from her all the time wonderful and sweet. When she looked at the house, she did a double-take.

"This is the Blaiser's place, and it's been abandoned for two years."

"How do you know that?" he asked.

"Carole Anne told me all about it one morning on our way to kick-boxing. We drive by it every day.'"

"Well, it's real cheap, and I figure I can fix it up."

"You figure you can?" She looked at him, her smile hopefully fun and flirtatious.

"You don't think I can fix up a house?"

"I have no idea what you can do, Dylan."

He snatched his phone from her, a devilish twinkle in his eye. "I think you have some idea, sweetheart." He wrapped both of his arms around her then, and she giggled and squirmed like she wanted to get away.

But she didn't. She wanted to stay in the safe circle of this man's arms for a long time. So she stilled, and his laughter died away too. Their eyes met, and he said, "I love you, Cami," in the most serious voice she'd ever heard him use.

"I—"

"Hey, you two."

Cami glanced out toward the front yard and saw Carole Anne and Levi standing there, hand-in-hand.

"Oh, hey." She straightened and ran her fingers through her hair. She wondered how she would've finished that sentence. Could she tell Dylan she loved him when she wasn't sure?

Help me figure out how I feel, she prayed as she stood and went down the steps to give her friend a hug.

"Everything go through okay with the loan?" Levi asked, and Cami nodded.

"Yep, all good. I probably won't purchase the business until the new year. That's what their offer was." She grinned at him. "But thank you for all your help on it." She turned back as Dylan came down the last couple of steps. "You guys know Dylan Walker."

"Of course." Levi shook his hand. "Well, we won't keep you."

"Oh, we're just decorating my tree," Cami said like it was no big deal. "Waiting for dinner to come."

As if summoned by her words, a car pulled into her driveway and the pizza delivery driver got out. Carole Anne and Levi went next door while Dylan paid, and by the time Cami was alone with Dylan again, way too much time had passed to return to that conversation on the front porch.

The one from the sleigh last week about having a family flooded her mind, and she realized with a jolt that Dylan was very, very serious about her.

She waited for the fear to come, but it didn't, and a small smile touched Cami's lips.

"What are you smiling at?" he asked as he set her salad in front of her.

"Nothing," she said. "Nothing at all. Thanks."

They ate, and the conversation went back to easy things. The Christmas parade and how the vehicles were coming along. His family pictures from earlier that day—and Cami didn't think she'd ever laughed as hard as she did at the things he said about his oldest sister and how yes, all of her kids had already cried before the photographer had even shown up.

He got up on the ladder and got the Christmas ornaments out of the attic, and she played holiday music while they dressed the tree up with lights and colored balls.

And when Cami stood next to Dylan, his arm around her shoulders, as they gazed at the lit tree, she couldn't remember a happier time in her life.

Thank you, she thought, the simplest but most sincere prayer she had to offer.

CHAPTER SEVENTEEN

"And I bought her a ring," Dylan said to Mint Brownie. He'd been talking to the horse for a solid half-hour. Everything about the sleigh talks he and Cami had, about the tree trimming experience from the other night, and then the trip to the jeweler.

"I'm in love with her." And he'd said it out loud to her. She'd looked like he'd just punched her with a brick, and she'd started to say something back to him.

That single "I—" had been haunting him for days, and while he'd never had a problem with Carole Anne or Levi, he wanted to ask them why. *Why* had they had to show up at that exact moment?

But he knew better than most that asking why was never a good idea.

Cami had retreated the teensiest little bit that night, but she'd sat beside him at church, as usual. Monday, she'd been silent, but Dylan couldn't blame her. She had a ton of work to do at Rivers Merge, and so did he.

With the Christmas parade only three days away, he also had all the last-minute checks to make on every single float. Oh, and one he hadn't even completely finished yet.

But he'd get it done, just like he always did. He was just a little busier this year because of the new build. But if there was one thing he'd learned over the years, it was that the work always got done.

That was what he'd told Bill and Patricia whenever they asked about the workshop. *I'll get it done.*

But it was a huge pain in the neck, and he still hadn't gotten all of the lights on the conveyor belt in the workshop to shine at the same time.

"How's he doing?"

Dylan glanced at Pete, glad he hadn't been confessing anything to Mint Brownie for the man to hear.

"Just great," he said, his focus switching from the horse to the veteran out in the arena. Jake rode a horse named Strawberry Shortcake, and he directed the red beast with only one hand.

"How are you?" Pete asked. "You don't stay for dinner anymore."

"Yeah," Dylan said, not wanting to get too far into his reasons for leaving as soon as he could on Tuesdays and Thursdays. He used to stay out at the ranch for a long time, even after the sessions ended. "I'm seeing Cami Cruz." He flashed Pete a smile. "So I head back to town right after I'm done here."

"I don't know Cami Cruz," he said, leaning his weight into the fence and continuing to watch Jake.

"She's the plumber for Rogers," Dylan said. "She's going to buy the whole operation come January." He couldn't help the pride that snuck into his voice. He cleared his throat, and asked, "Are you bringing the family in to the parade this weekend?"

"That's this weekend?"

"This weekend kicks it off," Dylan said. "And it runs next weekend, and then every night during the Twelve Days of Christmas."

Pete sighed. "I can't believe it's Christmas already. Where did this year go?"

"Not sure," Dylan said, feeling the way time passed through his fingers like smoke.

"Guess I better take the kids. They love the parade. And I need to get them some presents too, though Chelsea probably already has a bunch." He chuckled and Dylan smiled with him.

He hadn't thought much about presents yet either, as it was barely December and he didn't have a whole lot of people to buy for anyway.

"All right." Pete knocked on the wood. "You'll close up when he's done?"

"Sure thing." Dylan watched Pete walk away, his admiration for the man rising. He ran a good thing here and he managed to spend time with his family too, something that gave Dylan hope for him and Cami.

Dylan swung onto Mint Brownie and took the horse out into the arena with Jake and Shortcake. He hadn't ridden for a couple of weeks, and he moved Brownie through a few walking sequences, mostly to get his brain to stop circling Cami.

But she was always there, in his mind. He wanted to drive to her place after he brushed down both horses and made sure all the stalls in the stable were closed. But he pulled into his covered parking spot instead and sat in his truck.

He wanted to go into an apartment draped with garland and twinkling lights, preferably with hot food on the table and low music playing. And he knew he wouldn't get that inside his apartment.

So he pulled out his phone and called Boone. "Hey," he said when his friend answered. "I'm going to be buying a house soon. You got any dogs up for adoption at the clinic?"

"Lots," he said. "But they go fast in December. Lots of people adopt for Christmas."

"Mm." Dylan stared out the windshield, unable to pinpoint why his mood wasn't better this evening. He'd had a very productive day in the warehouse and then at Rivers Merge. He'd got to ride Mint Brownie and talk to Jake.

"How are things with Cami?" Boone asked. "Nicole wants to double."

"Sure," Dylan said, maybe a little too loudly. "We're going to the parade this Friday, if you guys want to come."

"You talk to her first," Boone said. "Besides, you'll be crazy-busy at that, with all the last-minute stuff you do."

"True," Dylan said, Boone's laughter breaking through his melancholy mood. "All right, if you see a good dog come in, save him for me."

"Will do."

Dylan hung up and he stretched across the cab and opened the glove box where he'd been hiding Cami's ring. He opened the black velvet box and gazed at the gem, his mood lifting further. He liked having a secret, something warm in his chest to buoy him up when he felt like he was the only man in Three Rivers who didn't have absolutely everything figured out.

He took the bag and box containing the ring with him as he headed for the front door of his apartment building. He waved to Mrs. Forrester as she came out of the pool area, and he rode the elevator to the sixth floor by himself.

Yes, his apartment was dark when he entered it, but it brightened with a few flips of a switch. He turned on the radio for companionship, and they were playing holiday songs, so he got his low music.

Instead of pulling out the bread and making a sandwich, he collected a roll of wrapping paper—the only roll of wrapping paper he owned—from the front hall closet.

It was red, with silver snowflakes on it, and he carefully wrapped the ring box, making sure to tape down all the finicky corners.

He stared at the tiny present, and he didn't like it. She'd know what it was the moment he presented it to her, making the wrapping job unnecessary.

So he unwrapped it and turned in a full circle in his kitchen, trying to think if he had any other boxes. He wasn't one to order much online, so he really didn't have anything shipped to him.

Now, the Electric Company had plenty of boxes, in all

shapes and sizes, as their equipment and bulbs were as various as the flowers on the earth.

So he'd wait. He was getting really good at that, and he tucked the ring box back inside the bag and set it on the shelf in the hall closet.

Cami didn't usually show up unannounced at his place, but he certainly didn't want her to see the box or the bag with the jeweler's insignia on it when she wasn't ready.

And he wasn't going to ask her to marry him until he knew she was ready.

"You're not," he told himself as he poured a bowl of cereal and parked himself in front of the TV. "You're really not."

∽

"TRY IT NOW," HE SAID TO BILL, PRESSING HARDER ON THE little clip of the last light bulb that was giving him fits. He'd replaced it twice, and if it didn't work this time, he thought he might just rip the light-up hammer out of Snoopy's hand.

"All right," Bill drawled, and it seemed like ten years passed for the man to walk around the float, lean in, and activate the mechanisms. Everything should move and light up this time, and with the parade only an hour away, Dylan didn't know what he'd do if it didn't.

But the green light came on, and Snoopy's hand swung down. Dylan whooped, and Cami started to laugh from where she sat in the sleigh, a folder of paperwork open in her lap.

When she'd arrived about twenty minutes ago, she'd told

him that she had about five hours worth of work to do in the last house. So she'd finish it all up tomorrow, and then they'd get a little breather before the holidays as other crews came in.

Well, not Dylan. He worked behind Cami in the new builds, and he still had plenty to do to get all the houses wired.

He stood back with Bill and Patricia, mentally congratulating himself for getting everything in tip-top shape for another parade.

He loved Three Rivers and the light parade it put on every year. Loved seeing the Clydesdales and sipping hot chocolate though it wasn't all that cold. He liked the festive atmosphere and the holiday vibe in the air as all the shops stayed open late and had sidewalk sales until nearly midnight on parade nights.

"Is that all?" he asked, turning as a loud metal screeching noise tore through the air.

"That'll be the drivers," Bill said. "Let's see what they say."

Another two big, huge, two-story garage doors opened, and more people came into the warehouse. Cami jumped down out of the sleigh and came over to Dylan.

"What's going on?" she asked.

"They're the drivers," he said. "They'll get instructions from Patricia, and then they'll test everything again. I make any last-minute fixes, and then we can hurry over to the parade route."

"Carole Anne is saving us a place," she said. "We don't have to hurry."

"Sure, we do," he said. "I don't want to miss any of the parade."

She looked at him for an extra-long moment, probably trying to figure out if he was kidding or not. He wasn't. The mayor led the parade in a bright, cherry-red Mustang, which blasted "Santa Claus is Comin' to Town" from the speakers, and Dylan loved it. He always had.

"My parents would bring us early," he told Cami, keeping one eye on the meeting with the drivers and Patricia. "We got to pick exactly one treat, and then we'd sit on blankets in the park for the parade." He swung his arm around her and brought her close to him, the folder the only thing between them. "Can you guess what I got for my treat?"

"Uh, let's see. Too cold for ice cream...." She grinned up at him, and dang, if Dylan didn't see at least the hint of love in her eyes. "And Christmas around here is a pretty big deal with the candied nuts. I'm going to go with that."

Dylan laughed. "Almonds. Cinnamon roasted almonds. I loved them, mostly because two out of my three sisters wouldn't touch them." He chuckled again, and the meeting broke up. "Oh, here they come."

He stepped away from Cami, but he didn't go far. She said, "I'm going to miss coming here and hanging out in that sleigh while you work." She slipped her hand into his and squeezed.

"Me too," he said. "But hey, we know where to find it, right?" He glanced at her, but he couldn't truly look as Bill called his name.

"Oh, boy," he said. "Be back in a minute."

At least twenty minutes passed before every driver was

satisfied with their floats. Dylan saluted to Bill and Patricia, took Cami's hand again, and said, "Let's get out of here while we can."

She giggled, and he practically ran toward the exit, pretending like they were sneaking away to steal a kiss. As they approached Main Street, he could hear the song blasting through the darkness, and he increased his pace.

"She's right there," Cami said, pointing to her right. She tugged on his hand, and he let her lead him through a throng of people to a couple of spaces next to Carole Anne and Levi.

"You made it," Carole Anne said, her face shining with Christmas spirit.

Dylan felt it infect him too, and he grinned as he turned his attention to the street in front of him. The mayor hadn't arrived yet, but he could hear him coming.

Everyone in town could, whether they were at the parade or not. Dylan grinned like he was six-years-old and it was Christmas morning as the red Mustang came into view.

The crowd, most of whom had been waiting longer than he had, started to cheer. The mayor waved from his position on the back of the Mustang, and the parade was off to a great start.

Dylan loved everything about this night, and he brought Cami closer to his side, pressed his lips against her temple, and said, "I'm so glad we're here together."

"Yeah, it can be a tradition," she said, causing him to look away from the league of toy soldiers marching in front of him.

"Yeah," he said slowly. "Our first Christmas tradition."

"No." She shook her head, those honeyed eyes glittering with all the lights from the parade. "That was when we put the tree up the day after Thanksgiving."

"Mm." He kissed her, glad when she pressed further into him, and then he watched the parade go by, happier than he'd ever been.

He could only hope and pray that Cami felt similar things for him. And though Dylan wasn't really the type to worry about things he couldn't control, a sliver of doubt crept in among the holiday joy, even when she jumped up and bought a sack of cinnamon almonds from a boy pulling a wagon down the side of the parade route.

CHAPTER EIGHTEEN

Cami entered Rogers Plumbing a week after the Christmas parade. And she thought the lights had been magical the first time she'd seen them. But nothing was the same when she was with Dylan. He made everything better, brighter, beautiful.

"Hey," she said when Dana looked up. "I have all the paperwork for you." She handed Dana the folder she'd taken everywhere with her for about two weeks now. "I've been over it all, and I think I've signed everywhere I need to."

She collapsed into the chair across from Dana, bone tired from the day's jobs. She hadn't even been up to the build since she finished the last house last weekend, but she'd need to get up there soon and pick up the specs for the next phase. Just the thought of looking at new specs made her eyes burn.

"Thanks," Dana said, and Cami gave her a weak smile.

"I'll have Abraham go over it with the lawyer, but I think we're all set for the purchase come January first."

Cami was too, but a flutter of nerves hit her. Dana wouldn't be working the desk anymore, and Cami suddenly realized she'd have to hire someone to run the office. Do the books. Make the appointments. Collect and deposit the money. Pay the bills.

And that meant someone she trusted and could work well with. She knew a lot of people in Three Rivers by face, but hardly any by name.

Her phone rang, interrupting her mounting panic, and she swiped on a call from Dylan with a quick wave to Dana. Her muscles protested as she stood, but she hobbled toward the front door anyway, saying, "Hey."

"Hey, pretty girl. Where you at?"

"Just leaving Rogers," she said, stepping onto the sidewalk and freezing. "Do you think I'll need to change the name?" There were so many things she hadn't thought of, and she felt like a fool.

"Not unless you want to. It's been Rogers Plumbing for something like forty years. People will still call it that anyway."

And she wouldn't have to pay to get a new sign made, repaint Penny, get new shirts, any of it.

"I'm calling because I've decided to get a dog," he said, his voice a bit louder than normal, like he was making an announcement.

"That's great," she said, because she knew he loved dogs and had wanted one for a while. "But I thought you weren't moving until January eighth." He'd bought the fixer upper a couple of blocks away from her house, and while it was nowhere near move-in ready, he claimed he could live there while he did some work.

She'd put him through the grinder with questions about the roof and what he'd do if it rained. He'd waved her away with, "It hardly ever rains here," and she'd asked him about new, energy-efficient windows, and hey, maybe a floor your foot didn't fall through would be nice.

"I'm not," he said. 'That's where you come in."

"Oh, I see where this is going already," she said, employing her professional tone, though he already knew she'd let him keep whatever pup he picked at her place until he moved. "And I don't like it."

"Please, Cami?" he asked. "Boone says they just got in a new litter of pups, and if I don't get one tonight, they'll be gone." His voice pitched up, but he cleared his throat. "All the moms will come take them for Christmas presents."

"So am I your mom?" she asked.

"No way," he said. "You're my girlfriend, who happens to have a great backyard for a dog. It's just a couple of weeks."

"It's like a month," she said. "And this is a *puppy*? It won't be potty trained?"

"It'll sleep outside."

"You're nothing but trouble, Dylan Walker."

He laughed, and she did too, and she finally got her feet moving toward Penny around the side of the shop. "I'm on my way over now, if you want to meet me there."

"I'm sitting in your driveway," he said. "Why don't you come home first, and then we'll go? I'll take you to dinner afterward."

She shook her head, though he couldn't see her, and said, "Sure. See you in a few."

He was indeed waiting in her driveway, so she pulled up to the curb and got out of the van. When she opened the passenger door and climbed into his truck, she said, "You realize you can't leave a puppy in here unattended while we go to dinner."

He blinked a couple of times, which made her laugh and shake her head again. "I don't think you've thought pet ownership all the way through."

"I have," he said. "Boone works all the time and he has two dogs."

"They probably go to work with him," she said. "And they're not puppies, and you babysit them all the time when he has to leave town." She slid across the seat and kissed him. "But come on, cowboy. You want a dog? Let's go get a dog."

The animal shelter wasn't too far from Cami's house, and Dylan parked toward the back entrance to the shelter. There were no other cars in the lot, and only the one window with any light.

"Are you sure they're open?" she asked, peering out of the windshield at the old building.

"Boone said he'd meet me here." He got out, and Cami followed him. The door was open, and sure enough, when they went in, Boone turned from the counter where he stood.

"Hey, guys." He flashed a smile at them and came closer. "You must be Dylan's Cami. I'm Boone Carver."

Dylan's Cami.

She liked the sound of that, and she instantly liked Boone too. He had a soothing way about him, from the huge cowboy hat on his head to the shiny shoes on his feet.

"Hey, man." He shoulder-clapped Dylan and added, "Puppies are over here." He led them to an enclosure where six dogs were living. Three or four of them got up and came over to the fence closest to Dylan and Boone, and Cami stayed back to watch.

"You want one who's interested in you," Boone said. "But not a barker. That big blackish one in the front, he's the pack leader. I'd go for one of the browner ones."

Dylan picked up the pack leader and cradled the dog against his chest. "German shepherds," he said to Cami as if she couldn't tell the most popular breed of dog just by looking.

She smiled but didn't crowd into the limited space. Dylan put the bigger, blacker dog down and picked up a brown one. The pup licked his face, and he laughed. Cami liked hearing his happiness, seeing the joy in his eyes, and she told herself it was worth having an un-potty trained dog in her yard for a month if Dylan wanted it.

And she knew, once again, that she was in love with him.

The real question now was: When could she tell him?

He hadn't told her again that he loved her, and she'd sort of been waiting for him to do that. Then she'd have an easy way to get her feelings out without having to bring it up.

"This one," Dylan said. "I want this one."

"What are you going to name him?" Boone asked, retreating to the spot where he'd left his clipboard on the counter.

Dylan looked at Cami, but she shrugged. "I'm not naming your dog."

"I don't know," Dylan said. "Let me think about it." He put the dog back in the enclosure with his siblings. "When will they be ready?"

"Next Friday," Boone said.

Dylan slung his arm around Cami's shoulders. "See? It really will only be a couple of weeks by the time we get to take him."

∽

Cami went out to Rivers Merge the next morning, bright-eyed and fresh from her kick-boxing workout. Her first job for Rogers wasn't until ten, and she figured the gym was closer to the build than her house, and she could get the phase two specs, and then head home to shower.

She found several trucks parked in front of the trailer, which was a bit odd for how early she was. But undaunted, she went up the steps and opened the door.

"She's here," someone said, but Cami couldn't identify who, as there were several men standing in the trailer, most of them with their back to her.

Gerald rose from the desk and everyone seemed to part and turn and look at her at the same time. Gerald wore an indiscernible look on his face. "Site five, six, and seven have flooded."

Horror infected Cami, from her toes to her forehead, as the words landed like bombs in her ears. She couldn't move. Couldn't speak. Her thoughts spun, trying to figure out what she'd done wrong in those three homes that she hadn't in the others. Her mind couldn't settle onto any one thought.

"We should've hired Wadsworth," someone said, a suit from the building company, and Cami finally got her neck to wrench in his direction.

"It's not too late," another man said.

Cami faced all men. Always all men.

"No," she managed to croak. "I didn't do anything wrong in the rough plumb of any of the sites."

Every eye stared at her, and she felt vastly outnumbered. But *she* was the right one for this job, and she wasn't going to let Wade Wadsworth come waltzing in here and take it from her.

"I saw Wade Wadsworth here at the trailer," she said. "A couple of months ago. Maybe longer than that. Maybe he came back and...." She trailed off, the thought too wild, even to attribute to Wade. But he had been here that day Dylan had brought her coffee, and that was when she'd plumbed those specific houses.

"What?" Suit One asked. "Sabotaged your work?"

Cami lifted her chin. "Yeah, something like that." She folded her arms. "I want to see the sites."

"I've got restoration crews in them already," Gerald said. "Water's all off. Power too."

"Power?" She glanced around for Dylan but he wasn't there. Why wasn't he there? But slowly her mind switched from Dylan to the real problem. "Those sites shouldn't have live power yet. Not until the drywall goes up and the furnace needs to kick on."

She thought back. She'd finished the last two homes

about ten days ago. The roofers had been taking two days to roof, and Dylan took a week to wire the whole house. So she finished a house one day, and Dylan finished with it a week and a half later.

So, yes, the power would be in sites five, six, and seven, but it shouldn't actually be live until the drywall went in, which didn't happen until after insulation, which hadn't even cleared site three yet.

"The only sites that should have live power are one and two," she said. "Why did five, six, and seven have it?"

"Who cares about the power?" Suit Two asked. "We're talking about water here." He waved his hands around like he was swimming. "*Water*," he said again, as if she was too stupid to understand him. "And that water is everywhere in those homes. The subfloors will need to be replaced, part of the walls. This is a huge problem, loads of money and work and...."

Cami hoped her glare had silenced him. "The power controls the—"

"Water pump," Gerald said with Cami.

"I want to see the sites," Cami said again, ready to die on this hill. "It's not my fault if the pumps came on when they weren't supposed to and flooded the houses. My job is to move the water from one place to another. It's everyone's job to make sure that doesn't happen until the right time."

Gerald collected a large ring of keys and moved toward her. "Let's go see the sites."

As they walked down the gravel paths that would become roads, Cami fired off a quick text to Dylan: *Where you at?*

Sick today. Couldn't stop puking last night.

Her heart went out to him, and she felt a tiny bit guilty for being mad at him that he wasn't there to support her. And that she'd practically thrown him under the bus. But she honestly couldn't think of a single thing she'd done to make all the pipes in the houses flood.

The restoration van had pulled all the way to the cement steps leading into the house, and two hoses—one red, one blue—snaked through the open front door of site five.

"Stan!" Gerald called, and the machinery roaring inside the house stopped. "What's the verdict?"

"We can get it dried out," he said. "There are some places that need to be replaced. We're testing the stability of them as we go and outlining the sections that will need to be redone."

Gerald nodded and looked around at the skeleton of the house. About six inches up the walls, the water line was evident. Cami stared at it in disbelief. This had been leaking for a long time.

She said so, and Gerald held up his hand. "Stan?"

"Yeah," Stan said, glancing around. "The pumps came on, oh, I don't know. I would guess early evening last night and ran all night."

Cami drew in a breath. Not her fault. Those pumps shouldn't have come on, not until the water lines were hooked up to appliances and drains.

"Why did the pumps suddenly come on?" Gerald asked. "This home's had electrical for a week."

"Dunno." Stan wiped his hand through his hair. "But that's what happened in all three houses."

"But not number eight?" Cami asked.

"That one's not done yet," Gerald said. "Dylan called in sick today, but he said he'd get the electrical in this week, on schedule."

"So it didn't flood. No power to the pump." Cami nodded like that solved the problem. "This has nothing to do with my plumbing work," she said.

No one with her—not Gerald, not Stan, neither of the two suits from Saddleback—looked as convinced as she was.

"Why don't you—?" Gerald started.

"I'll be getting the specs for phase two," she interrupted. "I have appointments all day today, and I don't have time for this." She stalked away, expecting him to call after her that she was fired, that she'd lost the bid, that they'd be calling Wade to come finish the rest of the phases.

He didn't, and Cami made it back to the trailer, her hands shaking with fury and fear. Now, if she just knew where the phase two specs were....

Only thirty minutes passed before Gerald and his posse came through the front door. This time, Dylan was with them. His skin looked like wet cement and sweat plastered his hair to his forehead. She wanted him to come to her side, *take* her side, but he just stood half a step behind Gerald, his eyes worried and his mouth closed.

She wouldn't beg him to come join her, though his name sat against the tip of her tongue to do exactly that. She bit back the urge and folded her arms.

"Just take today off," Gerald said. "Until we can figure out what to do."

"No." Cami shook her head. "You've already figured out

what to do. You hired a restoration company to fix the water damage."

"The water damage is going to cost twenty thousand to repair," Suit Two said.

"You have the money," she hurled back, appraising his clothes like they alone could make up the financial loss. For all she knew, they could.

Calm down, she commanded herself. Now wasn't the time for her temper to get the better of her. "I didn't do anything wrong," she said, hating the pleading note in her voice. She didn't want Dylan to get fired either, and she honestly didn't know why those pumps had come on last night. Her theory that Wade had come and played a little game of sabotage was sounding better and better with every breath she took.

Dylan should know she didn't do anything wrong. He wired in the same walls where she plumbed. He would've seen any mistakes. He'd have reported it, and she'd have fixed them.

He'd said nothing, just like he was now.

That hurt more than the thought of losing this bid.

"Cami," Gerald said, but she didn't hear his next words.

Losing Dylan hurt more than losing her job, and that had never been the case with anyone before. She stalked forward, ignoring Gerald and the Suits completely. She paused in front of Dylan, her emotion so close to the surface. So close.

"We're done," she bit out, stomping down the stairs and back to Penny.

She got out of the parking lot, away from Rivers Merge, before the first tears fell.

The following day, Cami had scheduled as many jobs as humanly possible. She'd spent her "day off" yesterday working for Rogers, just as she'd planned. But she hadn't gotten the phase two specs, and therefore, she didn't know what to expect once the New Year hit.

Heck, she didn't even know what to expect for today or tomorrow, not when it came to Rivers Merge.

So she spent her time with wrenches and pipes and toilets. They didn't betray her. Didn't spew hot water when they should be cold. Didn't ask her if she wanted kids when he wasn't serious. Didn't take her home to spend time with him, making traditions and telling her he loved her only to break her heart.

Cami had finally felt like her life was coming together into something she could be proud of. A new business. A new boyfriend.

Why did this have to happen now? she wondered, even tipping her head back to look at the ceiling.

God didn't answer, leaving Cami as frustrated and cranky as ever.

She finished the job, collected the check and signature on the work order board, and left the home only to find Dylan's shiny white truck parked across the street. Her traitorous feet slowed, and her hopeless heart thumped harder and harder.

She finally got herself moving toward Penny again. If she could just get inside, the van would protect her. Get her out of here.

"Cami," Dylan called as he got out of his truck.

She ignored him and wrenched open Penny's door, the metal squealing in protest. "Sorry," she muttered. "Sorry, sorry, sorry."

She was just about to yank the door closed when Dylan's strong hand stopped it. "I just want to talk to you."

"I don't care about anything you have to say," she said. Especially not now. Not when he hadn't said *anything* when it really mattered.

"They—"

"*¡Vete!*" she said in Spanish, lurching out of the car. *Go away!* She just wanted to get away. "*¡Déjame solo!*" She continued in Spanish, because each word seemed to knock Dylan back half a step. He finally moved enough for her to stalk back to the van and slam the door.

"Come on, Penny," she said, her voice shaking along with every muscle in her body. "Let's go."

CHAPTER NINETEEN

Dylan stared after the gray Rogers Plumbing van—Penny—his heart driving away with the woman behind the wheel. His head hurt; his throat hurt; he needed some pain medication and a dark room in which to take a nap.

But he stood on the street, his girlfriend having just whipped him in Spanish and then driven away. The jukebox incident from years ago filtered through his mind. But this time, he actually understood her frustration. Her fury.

What do I do now? he pleaded silently. He hadn't dared tell his mother about the break-up. Boone either, and by some slip of fate, they'd both called last night. Dylan had avoided his mother's call and gotten off the line with Boone after only twenty-four seconds.

With his heart cracked, he made his way back across the street to his truck. He had work to do too, and tracking

Cami down had taken a couple of hours that morning that he didn't have to spare.

He tried the last thing he had: his phone.

They aren't going to replace you on the build. I wouldn't let them. He sent the text and stared at his screen, willing her response to come back immediately.

How very noble of you, she sent. *It wasn't my fault those sites flooded. It was yours. And you just stood there and said nothing. You let me take the blame.*

Dylan's heart bounced around in his chest like it had been kicked. Was that true? Gerald hadn't said why the sites had flooded, only that they had, and he needed Dylan at the build site, puke or no puke. So Dylan had gone. He hadn't even seen the sites yesterday. Only the posse of men and the restoration van.

His plan to head home and get back to bed changed as he aimed his truck north toward Rivers Merge. His anger amplified with every second that passed where he didn't have the answers he needed. He hoped Gerald was at his desk, because if he wasn't, someone was going to have to weather a storm they didn't deserve.

He pushed into the construction trailer and found the foreman at his desk. Thankfully.

"Gerald," Dylan said. "How did those three sites flood?"

The foreman just gazed at him.

"Gerald." Dylan took careful steps forward. "It *was* Camila's fault, right? You wouldn't tell her something that wasn't true, right?"

Would he?

"That's not how we do things in Three Rivers," Dylan said when the foreman simply stared.

Gerald rolled his eyes. "When houses flood, it's a plumbing problem."

"No." Dylan shook his head. "There are a lot of reasons why a house might flood." Dylan's heart could barely beat. "She said it was my fault. What was she talking about?"

Gerald stood, sighed, and strode around his desk. "The water came on, because the pumps had power."

Dylan's confusion was complete, cascading through him like a waterfall. "No," he finally said. "I didn't connect the water pumps to power."

"Someone did."

"Who?" Dylan demanded.

"I don't know." Gerald stepped closer and then closer still. "So see? It was you or her, and it's not like I fired her. I'm planning to call her this evening and let her know everything has been cleared up and that I need her to get over here and get her specs so she can be ready to go."

"She'll be two days behind." Dylan just stared, his emotions all over the place, hardly able to be separated or defined.

"I'm going to offer to bring in a crew to help her."

Dylan's eyebrows sprang up. "A crew?" She wouldn't like that. Not one little bit.

"We need a few extra hands to get the flood-damaged wood fixed anyway, and those homes have to be rewired in spots, so you'll need the help—"

"I don't need any help." Apparently Dylan didn't like the thought of working with a crew of Gerald's men either. "And

I'm going to figure out who connected the water pumps to power." He turned and reached for the door handle.

"Dylan, if you do that—"

He spun back, his own anger shooting through his head, making it hard to order his words. "I'm not taking the blame for it, and Cami certainly shouldn't have to." He walked forward one slow step at a time. He paused when he was only a few feet from Gerald. "Just because she's a woman."

Gerald flinched, not the answer Dylan wanted. But at least he knew now why the blame had been pinned on Cami. He vowed he'd never tell her—but he guessed she knew already.

He went home, his mind churning. How could he find out who had connected those pumps to the power, who had ruined three sites, and who wanted Cami to take the fall for it?

Too riled up to sleep, he took several painkillers and pulled out his tiny tree for the coffee table. Three feet tall and pre-lit, he got it set up in under five minutes, tired of coming home to darkness and silence. He had one box of Christmas balls, and he hooked those onto the boughs in another five. Anything to keep his mind working, thinking through the problem.

He had exactly one gift to put under his Christmas tree this early. Cami's ring box. Profound sadness sang through him as he cracked the lid and looked at the diamond. Would he ever be able to give it to her? Would she even open the door if he went over there? How could he get her back?

Figure out who connected power to the pumps.

He wasn't sure if it was his thought, or that from a

Higher Power, but he knew he needed to do it if he wanted Cami in his life. And he did.

Help me, he pleaded. *Just give me a direction. The first step. Anything.*

Like lightning striking, an idea entered his mind. He reached for his phone, his heart pounding. With a froggy voice and an ache still pounding behind his eyes, he dialed the Sheriff's office.

He wasn't expecting the Sheriff himself, Brian Bellsby, to answer, but the man said, "Sheriff Bellsby here," like he spent all day answering phones.

"Sheriff Bellsby," Dylan said. "This is sort of an odd question, but do we have security cameras around town? Maybe something that tracks traffic or...?" Dylan couldn't really imagine there were cameras in Three Rivers, but it was the only thought that had come to his mind.

"We've got 'em around town, yeah," the Sheriff said. "Up on some of the street lamps."

Dylan's head felt light, almost detached from his body. "Up at the northern end of town?"

"Oh yeah. The residents up there have money, and they like the cameras."

"How can I get a look at the footage?" Dylan asked, wondering if there was some permit he needed, or a stack of papers he'd need to sign until his hand cramped.

"Why?" Dylan could practically see the older man lean forward, his eyes narrowed. He had the suspicious tone down pat.

Dylan didn't see a reason not to be truthful. "Three of

the houses at the Rivers Merge development were vandalized night before last."

"Vandalized? No one called in any vandalism."

"We thought it was a...an electrical mistake. I just learned today that it wasn't." That sounded reasonable, and it was true.

"If you'll come on down to the station, I'll get you the papers you need, and we'll pull the tapes."

Yep, paperwork. Not Dylan's strong suit. But one glance at the ring box sitting under his Christmas tree, and he said, "I'll be right over."

∽

An hour later, Dylan had practically signed enough papers to donate a kidney, and Sheriff Bellsby still hadn't gotten up from the desk. He looked at the last document very carefully, like Dylan had forged it right in front of him.

"It can take some time to locate the footage." Sheriff Bellsby finally stood, a long groan coming from his mouth.

"How much time?" Dylan asked.

"An hour or two."

Dylan checked his phone and saw it was almost lunchtime. "I'll be back then." He got up and left the police station to walk down the block to a diner that had been around as long as the town. The diner was hopping with noon customers, and Dylan joined the fray at the bar. He ordered a cheeseburger and fries and hoped he wouldn't see his boss from the Electric Company. He'd called in sick, and he wasn't sure how he'd explain his lunch downtown if Asher walked in.

Thankfully, he didn't, but another man sat down next to him. Dylan glanced at him and looked away when he didn't recognize him immediately.

"Hey, Dylan."

He turned back to the man. "Oh, uh...Thomas, right?" He was the architect on the build, but Dylan hadn't seen him since he'd announced the bid winners, months ago.

"Right." He flashed Dylan that icy smile and ordered coffee and a Reuben sandwich from the waitress as she walked by.

"What brings you here?" Dylan asked as his food arrived. He busied himself with his burger, but that same slinky feeling crawled over his skin at Thomas's proximity.

"Looking at the flooded houses," he said. "Assessing the damage."

Dylan took a bite of his cheeseburger, his mind spinning. He decided to simply be frank. He put down his burger and took a long drink of his sweet tea. "Why would the architect need to assess the flood damage on the build? You design the houses, right? Isn't your job long done?"

Thomas trained his blue eyes on Dylan's, lasers practically shooting from his gaze. "I have a keen interest in Rivers Merge."

"You do?" Dylan leaned onto one elbow and faced Thomas fully. "What is it?"

"It's private." He turned his attention to his coffee and spooned sugar into the black brew, his demeanor closed and tight.

"Where does your family live now?" Dylan turned back to his food, but his appetite had vanished.

"Austin," he said.

"And you?"

"I have offices in a couple of places."

Dylan heard the evasion in the man's voice. He took another good look at him, wondering if he'd see the man's face on the surveillance footage.

Thomas's food arrived, and he said, "Can I actually get it to go?"

Dylan saw his window of opportunity shrinking, but he couldn't think of any more questions to ask short of accusing Thomas of connecting the water pumps to the power supplies.

"What's your sister doing these days?" he asked instead, the question just there for some reason.

"Lydia?"

"No, the one just younger than you. She was my age, wasn't she?"

Thomas's face hardened and his jaw jumped as he clenched his teeth. "Maisie. She, uh." He cleared his throat and accepted the Styrofoam container with his sandwich inside. He looked right at Dylan, his gaze piercing and sending a liquid chill through Dylan. "She passed away about ten years ago."

Dylan flinched as regret lanced through him. "I'm so sorry."

"Yeah." Thomas stood and walked toward the cash register, leaving Dylan to wonder what had just happened. He had more questions now than answers, and he mulled through everything he knew about the Martin family—which admittedly wasn't much.

He wondered how much information the Internet could provide, and he added it to his day's to-do list as he mixed mustard and ketchup to make an orange sauce for his French fries.

After he finished eating, he headed back to the police station, where he found Sheriff Bellsby with a grumpy look on his face.

"What is it?" Dylan asked as he approached, his steps slowing the closer he got to the Sheriff.

"There was just a man here, asking about the exact same tape you were."

"Who was it?" He braced himself to hear the name Thomas Martin.

"A guy by the name of Wade Wadsworth." The Sheriff paced, his frown stuck in place.

"Well, you didn't give it to him, did you?"

"He said he was workin' with you." The Sheriff finally met Dylan's eyes, panic and understanding parading through his expression at the same time. "He's not workin' with you, is he?"

"I don't even know who Wade—" His voice muted. He *did* know who Wade Wadsworth was.

Cami's abusive ex-boyfriend.

He spun, his heart jackhammering in his chest. "Can you come with me to Rogers Plumbing?" He dashed for the door, not bothering to wait for the Sheriff to come.

"Why?" The older man puffed as he came outside with Dylan.

"Wade is Camila Cruz's ex-boyfriend. She could be in danger."

"Where is she?"

"Probably out on a job." He headed for his truck. "Let's go ask Dana at the plumbing shop." He hated waiting for the slower Sheriff to climb into the truck, not when Cami could be in danger, not when Wade had the tape that could exonerate them both, not when Dylan felt like his entire life was hanging in the balance.

CHAPTER TWENTY

*C*ami went through the motions of twisting off water mains, fixing the leaks, the faucets, the toilet seals, whatever the job required. She missed the *blingy beep* of her phone, alerting her to a text. She missed her ongoing conversations with Dylan, and she looked forward to seeing him after work, sharing her life with him.

But her afternoon was silent except for the labored sound of her own breathing, and the scratching of pens as citizens wrote checks to pay for her services.

She'd just finished at an apartment in the building next to Dylan's, her arms loaded with her heavy equipment, when she burst out into the sunlight.

Squinting, she noticed two figures standing next to Penny. She automatically stopped, though her arms screamed at her to *hurry up and put down this toolbox!*

"Cami!" Dylan waved at her as if she couldn't see him. He

hurried toward her and took the heavy tools from her. "Are you okay?"

"Why wouldn't I be?" She glanced past him to find the Sheriff a few steps away. "What's going on?"

"Wade's in town," Dylan said as Sheriff Bellsby arrived. "Have you seen him?"

Cami's insides iced despite the warm afternoon. "Not today."

"When's the last time you saw him, ma'am?" the Sheriff asked.

"A few weeks, maybe a month, ago." Cami swallowed as she looked from Dylan to Sheriff Bellsby. "He was leaving the build site at Rivers Merge. I hid in my van until he left." She'd never told Dylan about her sighting of Wade. She didn't think it necessary.

"He took the surveillance footage of the build site." Dylan exhaled and turned away from her, wiping his hand through his hair. "I can't believe this."

"Do you think it was him?"

"I don't know." Dylan looked like a lost child, and the agony in his eyes made Cami's heart squeeze tight. Too tight.

"But someone hooked the pumps to the power, and it wasn't me and it wasn't you."

Pieces clicked around in Cami's head. He was trying to make it right. Figure out who had sabotaged those three houses. Clear her name.

A swelling of love filled her, and her throat turned thick.

"I'll find him," Sheriff Bellsby said. In the next moment, he had his radio off his hip and was speaking police codes into it at a rapid clip.

"Dylan," she started.

"Later, Cami." He gave her a half-daggered look and followed the Sheriff back to his truck. "Well, c'mon!" he called back to her.

"I have Penny."

Dylan practically stomped back to her. "I'm not letting you out of my sight, not even for a ten-minute drive back to the police station. Penny can stay here. She likes it here." He grabbed her hand and towed her after him.

"Dylan." She shook her hand out of his but kept going. "I'm fine."

"Your abusive ex-boyfriend is in town, and he lied to the Sheriff so he could get that tape." Dylan's brilliant blue eyes shone like glass. "Please, Cami. Don't make me beg you. Just get in the truck and stay by me, okay?"

She wanted to apologize. Wanted to tell him she loved him for what he'd done and what he was doing. Wanted to stretch up and kiss him, transfer some of her fear onto him. He'd take it, she knew. And he'd take it gladly.

Instead, she slipped past him and climbed into the truck, sandwiching herself between Dylan and the Sheriff for the ride back to the police station.

She called her remaining two appointments for the day and explained something had come up and she wouldn't be able to make it. Dylan didn't get out of the truck at the police station, but simply dropped off the Sheriff.

"Where are we going?" Cami asked.

"My apartment." He worried his lip between his teeth, something she'd never seen him do. In fact, this was the very first time Dylan had ever been anything less than cool and calm and collected.

And that scared her more than anything. This was real.

"Gerald isn't going to fire you or replace you," he said as he drove. It seemed like his mouth needed something to do to calm his nerves. "He still wants you to finish the build. Said to come get your specs."

Her blood started to boil, and Cami folded her arms to try to contain her annoyance.

"He knows—*everyone* knows—it wasn't your fault those houses flooded. I didn't realize they were blaming you, Cami. I swear I didn't. When I found out, I did the only thing I could think of—I went to the police and asked if there was any way that area had been recorded."

Her emotion welled inside her, causing her chin to shake and her eyes to sting with unshed tears.

"And Sheriff Bellsby said it would take a couple of hours to pull the tape, so I went to the diner. And Thomas was there—and that guy's creepy. He's got something going on with him, but I don't know what." He sighed as he turned into the parking lot at his building. "Anyway, when I got back to the station, the Sheriff said Wade had taken the tape. Claimed to be working with me and took the tape."

He parked a little roughly and got out of the truck without a pause. She followed him, glad when he waited for her. He didn't reach for her hand, though, and the loss of his touch tortured her. She walked a few steps behind him, hung out at the back of the elevator, and stepped off to suffocating silence.

He unlocked his door and went inside, locking them back behind the solid wood. "Did you eat lunch?"

She hadn't, but she couldn't stand to have him cook for her. Honestly, he wouldn't cook, but she didn't want him to go to any extra trouble because of her. He'd already done so much.

Her eyes landed on his Christmas tree. "You have a tree up?" At only three feet, it hardly counted as a tree, but still. She wandered over to it.

"Just trying to keep busy," he said. "That tree inspired me to call the Sheriff, so you best be nice to it."

Cami smiled at his cowboy drawl. Though he didn't wear his hat at the moment, he was a Southern boy through and through. *Her* Southern boy.

She touched a red ball on the tree limb, and her gaze drifted to a ring box sitting on the table under the tree. She reached for it at the same time Dylan lunged toward her. "Don't touch that." He sounded panicked, and she jerked her hand back like the ring box would electrocute her. He was an electrician, after all.

"What is it?"

He almost leapt over the couch and swiped the ring box away. "It's a gift."

"For who?" Cami eyed the box as he hid it behind his back.

He stared at her, sheer determination in his eyes. In a single breath, his demeanor changed and he brought the box out from behind him. "For you."

Cami's entire body lit up. He'd bought her a ring? What

kind of ring? And how should she react when he gave it to her?

He set it back on the table under the tree. "It's for later."

"Later?" Not the answer she wanted, and her curiosity carved a hot path through her bloodstream. She collapsed on the couch. "Dylan, I'm really sorry about this morning."

He sat tentatively beside her. "You believe me when I say I didn't know how the homes had flooded, right?"

She looked at him, right at him. "Of course." She sighed and dropped her eyes to his carpet. "You know I have a bad temper, right?"

His arm broke the physical barrier between them, sliding across her back and settling over her shoulders. "I like your fire, Cami."

"Fire burns."

"I'm used to dealing with electricity. I can handle you."

"I'm water; you're electricity. We don't go together."

He put his hand under her chin and gently pushed it up, forcing her to face him. "We absolutely belong together."

Those pesky tears burned her eyes now. "I really am sorry."

"I know you are." He gave her that swift, sexy, perfectly in control smile she loved so much. "We're going to figure out what happened at Rivers Merge."

"Thanks for that," she said, laying her head on his shoulder. "You sure I can't see the ring right now?"

"How do you even know it's a ring?"

She rolled her eyes. "I've seen ring boxes before."

He chuckled and ran his lips along her browline. "It's a Christmas gift," he said. "You'll have to be patient."

His phone sounded, the crack of a baseball bat echoing through the apartment, and he reached for it. "It's Sheriff Bellsby." He stood, his eyes shining as he read. "He found Wade." He was already moving toward the door. He had it open before he realized she wasn't with him. "You're not coming?"

"I haven't seen Wade in four years," she said, a slight tremor in her chest that matched the one in her voice.

"You don't have to be afraid of him."

"I'm not afraid of him." She shook her head. "I'm afraid of myself. Of what I'll do to him."

"You won't do anything," Dylan said. "You're not that kind of person." He reached for her hand, and she stepped over to him to slip her fingers through his. She went with him, down the elevator, into the truck, his words tumbling around inside her head.

She wasn't a malicious person. She hadn't gone after Wadsworth Plumbing after she'd been forced to quit. And she'd had cause. No, she simply wanted to move on with her life, find somewhere to belong.

And she had. Not only did she belong in Three Rivers, she belonged to Dylan Walker.

He pulled into the police station and started to get out, but she put her hand on his arm. "Wait."

He turned back to her, an expectant look on his face. "Yeah?"

"Before we go in there, I need you to know something."

"All right."

She twined her fingers through his again, looking at their joined hands. Warmth filled her, and sweet peace, and freeing forgiveness. "I love you, Dylan." Feeling brave and empowered, she looked up into his face.

He blinked once, twice. "I'm sorry. It sounded like you said you loved me."

She smiled and swatted his chest. "Come on."

He leaned close, closer, his eyes crinkling with a smile. "I love you too, Camila." His eyes drifted closed, and Cami dropped her gaze to his lips. Then she kissed him, pressing right into him and taking her time to explore his mouth.

He ducked his head and chuckled. "Okay, so that's out of the way. Let's go see who sabotaged those houses."

CHAPTER TWENTY-ONE

Dylan's step felt like he was walking on marshmallows. Cami's hand in his seemed like magic, and it wasn't until he pushed into the police station that he remembered why they were there.

Sheriff Bellsby waved to them from the mouth of a hallway, and Dylan led Cami in that direction. "Did you get the tape?" he asked the Sheriff when he was close enough.

"I'm afraid not." Sheriff Bellsby looked halfway between angry and annoyed. "And the man's not talking."

Frustration rose through Dylan. He just wanted to know who'd tried to get Cami fired. Or maybe they were trying to get him fired. Either way, he didn't like not knowing. Didn't like that Gerald didn't really care who was at fault.

Her phone rang at that moment, and she pulled it from her purse. "It's Gerald."

"I already told you what he's going to do," Dylan said.

"I'm going to take it anyway." She swiped on the call. "Hello, Gerald." She walked away from Dylan and the Sheriff.

"Didn't you say she has some sort of history with Wadsworth?"

"Her ex."

"He asked for her."

Dylan's heartbeat rippled like a flag in a stiff wind. "She's not going in there alone."

"Funny you should say that. He specifically requested she go in there alone."

Dylan started shaking his head before the Sheriff stopped speaking. "No. Wade was abusive. He'll—"

"He's handcuffed. He can't hurt her."

Still, Dylan didn't like the idea of Cami being thrown to a wolf. Didn't like it at all.

She returned, a half-smile on her face. "You were right. Now I have six days to get all the gear I need for phase two." Her mouth was tight and she shook her head.

"I'll help you," he said. "Sheriff Bellsby has some good news and some bad news."

The Sheriff looked at him in surprise. "I do?"

"Yeah, and they're the same. Wade's asked to see you alone."

Cami's eyebrows rose. "Is that the good news or the bad news?"

"It's both." Dylan sighed. "See what you can get him to tell us about the tape, the flooding, any of it." He stepped closer to her and dropped his voice. "You know him. He hasn't changed since you guys dated." He skated his lips across her temple, almost hating himself when he added, "Push his buttons. Get him to talk."

He pulled back and gazed at Cami, hoping she'd see and feel his desperation. They needed that tape, and Wade was their only link to it.

She nodded, the understanding and spark between them as strong as ever. "Where is he, Sheriff?"

Sheriff Bellsby lectured her about how far to stay from Wade, but that she wasn't in any danger—he and his officers would be right outside, the conversation would be recorded, the whole nine yards.

Dylan couldn't detect an ounce of insecurity in Cami as she stepped up to the one-way glass and looked into the room where Wade sat. She held very still, and Dylan didn't think he could stand to see her go in there with Wade alone.

She finally turned toward the Sheriff. "I'm ready." She didn't look at Dylan, didn't even so much as twitch toward him, before walking into the room.

"We'll be able to hear her, right?" Dylan rushed toward the glass, his eyes only trained on Cami.

His question was answered when she said, "Hello, Wade," and he could hear her voice, albeit tinny and stretched thin.

Wade didn't answer, and Cami gave him a wide berth as she pulled out the chair opposite him and sat down. "What brings you to Three Rivers?"

Still nothing.

"I saw you at the bidding for Rivers Merge. You lost."

His face twitched the tiniest bit, and Dylan volleyed his

gaze back to Cami. She sat with her arms folded, her face expressionless. He didn't like this version of her. This masked, emotionless version.

"And then you came back." She leaned forward and put her hands on the table. "I saw you at the build site. It was strange, because you'd lost, and yet you had folders of information."

He blinked. She blinked back.

"You flooded those homes, didn't you?"

"No."

At least she'd gotten him to talk.

She gave a mirthless laugh that chilled Dylan's blood. "Yes, you did. We'll get that tape and see you on it, and then you won't be able to lie anymore."

"The tape is gone."

"Right," she said. "Just like you promised you'd never come to Three Rivers. By my count, you've been here three times. Today's visit makes it four, and I'm willing to bet there are more."

"Cami," he said, and Dylan never wanted him to say her name again. His fists curled at his sides and he worked to unfurl them.

He shook his head, the softness that had entered his face evaporating.

"What is it, Wade?" She leaned closer, and Dylan's internal alarms went off.

"Scoot back," he whispered, keeping a close eye on Wade.

Wade looked at the one-way glass and said, "Look up the architect. That's all I'm going to say." He pressed his lips together, and Cami waited several long seconds before standing.

She rejoined them in the hall, a sigh heaving from her chest. "He means it when he says that's all he's going to say."

"Who's the architect?" Sheriff Bellsby asked.

"Thomas Martin," Dylan said, his mind whirring. "He lived here in Three Rivers until he was twelve. He was at the diner at the same time as me. We talked for a few minutes, then he got his food to go, and he left." Dylan watched Wade behind the glass, slumped at the shoulders.

"I get a weird vibe from Thomas," Dylan said. "I can't put my finger on it, but there's something not right about him."

"Maybe he was at the diner with you to make sure Wade had enough time to get the tape." Cami looked at him with hope in her eyes. "Maybe they're working together."

"Not if Wade just named him," Sheriff Bellsby said. "Let me get my men on finding this Thomas Martin fella."

"That won't be necessary."

Dylan spun to find Thomas standing right behind him, a small tape in his hand. "I believe you were looking for this." He extended the tape to the Sheriff but he never tore his disgruntled gaze from Cami.

Who was he? Why didn't he like Cami? Why had *he* announced the winning bids and not Gerald, who had to work with all the winners? Dylan couldn't answer any of his questions.

Things happened fast after that. Dylan and Cami went with the Sheriff to a viewing room, while Thomas was taken to a holding room until they could question him.

Sheriff Bellsby put the tape in and told the technician to find Sunday evening. They watched in fast-forward until the sun set.

"There," the Sheriff said, but the technician had already slowed the footage. A plain, unmarked, white van pulled up to the curb, parking halfway out of the frame.

It didn't matter that they couldn't see the plate. Wade Wadsworth's face was extremely recognizable as he got out of the van and opened the back. He collected some tools and made his way onto the build site, first entering homesite five. Then six. Then seven.

"He's our guy," Sheriff Bellsby said. He left Dylan and Cami sitting in the tiny tech room.

"How does Thomas play into this?" Dylan asked.

She looked as perplexed as he felt.

Maisie.

Dylan pulled out his phone, saying, "Stupid."

"What?" Cami asked, peering at his screen as he pulled up an Internet browser.

"At the diner, I asked about his sister. He said she'd passed away. I thought I should look her up, but I didn't have time." He tapped and waited for the pages to load.

He found her obituary—and several other articles about doctor incompetence. He only had to scan a few lines of the article to know what was going on.

"Cami," he said. "Your brother was sued for medical malpractice in the death of Maisie Martin."

He looked up as if in slow motion. Cami stared at him in the same dream-like way. Then everything rushed forward again. "Let me see." She snatched the phone from his hand and her eyes flipped left and right as she read.

"So he's here for revenge," she said, her face a mask of agony. She'd told Dylan she didn't talk to her brother much—at least beyond arguing over fair wages for women.

In a single breath, her tortured expression dissolved, replaced with the fire Dylan often saw in her. "But what does Wade have to do with it?"

"He's the grunt man," Dylan said, shrugging. "He's probably getting paid a lot of money, and he's been promised that once you're gone, he'll get the bid on the rest of the phases."

"Why not just give it to him, if that's what Thomas wanted to do?"

"This way hurts more. Discredits you. Could ruin you right when you're buying the business here." Dylan was just guessing. He honestly didn't know why Thomas was so upset. It sounded like his sister had come into the emergency room with a five percent chance of living after a devastating car accident.

"The charges were dismissed," Cami said, her gaze dropping back to the dark screen.

"It's been ten years," Dylan said.

She lifted her eyes to his. "A long time to plan to ruin me, a woman who barely talks to her brother."

"I called a friend in Amarillo to come question Thomas," Sheriff Bellsby said. "He's just arrived and been briefed." He gestured for them to follow him, and Dylan tucked Cami's hand in his as they went to another room with a one-way window.

Two men went into the room where Thomas stood

staring at them through the window. He turned toward the pair of detectives, his face a placid mask of non-emotion.

Introductions were made. Small talk happened. Finally one of the detectives—a man named Detective Forge—sat at the table though Thomas hadn't yet. "So tell us about the tape you gave to Sheriff Bellsby."

"Wade Wadsworth brought it to the Rivers Merge build site and gave it to the construction foreman, Gerald Burnis. He claimed I had hired him to flood those three houses, which is preposterous." He sank into the chair opposite Detective Forge. "I designed the entire development. Why would I sabotage thirty percent of the progress?" He spread his arms wide, his voice incredulous.

Dylan knew he had a piece of paper declaring him an architect, but the man was also an excellent actor—and an absolute liar.

"He's lying," he whispered to Cami.

She turned to him, and he could see the wheels of her mind turning in her eyes. "He hired exclusively Three Rivers tradesmen. What if he's trying to sabotage all of us for some reason?"

Dylan searched her expression as he tried to imagine why anyone would do that. "He'd need a really good reason for that."

"We'll find out what it is," the Sheriff said. "Why don't you two get on out of here?" He cut a glance to the one-way window. "I have a feeling these two men will open up more without you here."

Dylan wanted to argue, wanted to stay and make sure the

person responsible for the flooding was punished, but he turned away.

Wasn't up to him. And he still needed a nap so he could finish all the work he'd fallen behind on.

He got his nap—with Cami in his arms and that ring box staring him in the face.

CHAPTER TWENTY-TWO

Cami called in her emergency plumbing crew, and together with Abraham and Raul, she managed to get the parts and equipment she needed for phase two of Rivers Merge.

She worked hard not to call the Sheriff every day, and as more days passed and she spent every evening after work with Dylan, she didn't realize she hadn't been updated in the case in over a week.

A detective hadn't come to see her, ask her any questions. Gerald acted like he hadn't accused her of flooding three houses. The Suits from Saddleback avoided her eyes whenever she crossed paths with them.

Cami didn't care. She'd stood up for herself when she'd needed to, and she'd been right. Dylan had returned to her side, but she disliked going to his apartment and had taken to inviting him over to sample some of her Mexican cooking.

After all, that ring box just sitting under his tiny Christmas tree drove Cami toward the edge of insanity.

He came willingly, never questioning why she'd stopped wanting to come to his place. Cami hummed as she put a can of crushed tomatoes and a can of corn in her Spanish rice, stirring as Dylan burst through the door.

"Have you heard?"

She spun from her spot at the stove. "Heard what?"

"Thomas Martin's father, Raston Martin, was found guilty of fraud and money laundering while he worked as the town's accountant. That's why they left town when Thomas was only twelve."

Cami's heart raced at the news. "So you think he was—?"

"I think he was going to discredit all of us. Sheriff Bellsby found a folder in his office in Amarillo that had the full build schedule, with notes about when plumbing would be done, and HVAC, and electrical...." Though his eyes shone, Dylan's voice held a horrified tone.

Cami left her rice to simmer and crossed the room to him. "What did he think would happen? We'd all go out of business?"

"He had other companies—Amarillo companies who didn't win the original bid—listed in the margins of the schedule."

Cami couldn't understand the level of pain and desperation Thomas must've felt in order to organize something so elaborate. "Has he admitted anything?"

"No, but Wade's story fits with the Sheriff's theory."

Feeling tired after weeks of work and worry, Cami sank onto her sofa. "Wow."

Dylan joined her, threading his fingers through hers. "Yeah. Wow."

They existed together in companionable silence. So companionable, Cami leaned into his body and laid her head on his shoulder.

"Hey, you're coming to Christmas Eve dinner at my parents', right?"

"Wouldn't miss it," she murmured.

"My mother asked you to bring tamales."

Cami glanced up at him. "She did?" From what she'd observed and been told, only Alecia brought food to the family dinners. Sally had claimed she didn't care—"Less work for me," she'd said—but Cami had seen the discomfort and jealousy on her face.

"I couldn't stop talking about them." Dylan grinned and pressed a kiss to the tip of her nose.

"What's everyone else bringing?" she asked.

His face blanked. "I have no idea."

Cami straightened. "Well, I'm not bringing something if no one else is."

"Why not?"

"Because it will hurt your sisters' feelings."

Dylan frowned. "What are you talkin' about?"

"Only Alecia brings food to the family dinners." She sighed at the fact that he didn't know this. "So I'm not bringing tamales if Sally and Rose aren't bringing something. I don't want to hurt their feelings."

"Only Alecia brings food to the family dinners?" Dylan asked.

Cami sighed. "I'll call your mom and ask her what

everyone else is bringing." She snuggled back into him. "When do you want to exchange gifts?"

"You got me something?"

"Duh," she said with a giggle as his lips trailed across her earlobe. "You've got that fancy-schmancy ring box still sitting under your tree."

"Maybe that's not for Christmas." His husky voice sent shivers through her, but she bolted upright anyway.

"Not for Christmas?" Her voice could've called dogs. "Dylan," she whined.

He grinned at her, his usual calm and cool self. Leaning back into the couch, he lifted his arm along the back of it. "You want that ring, huh?"

"I'd like to see it, yes." Was it made with diamonds? Cami sure hoped it was, but she was prepared for anything. She hoped.

"We can exchange gifts just before the dinner if you want." He reached for her and she melted into his embrace, kissing him in a way she hoped told him she really wanted a diamond from him.

∼

CHRISTMAS EVE FOUND HER IN THE ELEVATOR, ON HER way up to Dylan's apartment, her stomach a jittery mess of nerves. Her gift came in an equally small package as his—the receipt for At Bat Premium, a service that would allow him to watch every baseball game, everywhere, all the time.

Dylan was incredibly hard to shop for, but she'd spent a

few nights curled into his side while he watched baseball, and she hoped he'd like the subscription.

She knocked and entered his apartment as he came down the hall from his bedroom. "Hey." He leaned against the wall and scanned her, the way he always had. "No wonder my mother loves you."

She glanced down at her black pencil skirt and bright Christmas-red ribbed sweater, a smile forming on her face.

"I clean up nice." He wore a pair of gray slacks and a navy blue polo with thin white stripes on the upper half. "So do you." She moved into his embrace, inhaling that "toxic spill" cologne that had captured her attention from the start.

She kissed him, and he kissed her back, both hands sliding into her hair. Cami pulled away first, her jitters amplified by her worries about her gift. "Let's get this over with."

"Over with?"

"My gift is really lame." She pulled out the jewelry box she'd bought at the drugstore and stuffed the receipt into. "But I thought you'd like it, and—" She stopped talking. She was justifying her gift, and she hated that.

He took the box, which she'd covered in silver paper, and pulled the wrapping off. He lifted the lid and made a huge show out of unfolding the paper.

"At Bat Premium." A smile exploded across his face, and a laugh followed soon after that. "I've always wanted this."

He swept her off her feet, still chuckling. "Thank you, sweetheart. This is perfect." He set her back on her heels and moved over to his tree to collect the box.

Relief rushed through her for a few moments.

Then he dropped to one knee.

Tears sprang to her eyes. "Dylan," she said in a warning tone.

"Camila," he said back, cool, even, calm. "I'm in love with you. I can't imagine anyone else I'd like to spend my life with." He cracked the lid to reveal a baseball-shaped diamond that caused Cami's heart to quiver.

"Will you marry me?"

It was her turn to beam and laugh and shriek, "Yes," before launching herself into his arms. "I love you," she whispered into his ear.

"That's the only Christmas present I need." He pulled back and gazed at her. "But I'll take the baseball subscription too."

She giggled as he removed the ring from the box and explained the two bands. "So I keep this one, and you wear this one. When we're married, they get reunited." He slid the diamond on her left ring finger, and Cami had never thought she could be as happy as she was in that moment.

He kissed her again and said, "Let's go tell my family."

Cami held onto him for an extra beat, then two, then three.

"Cami?" he asked.

She sniffed and tried to wipe her eyes before he saw, but she couldn't. He watched her with curiosity. "I like this softer version of you," he whispered, taking her hand away from her face. "Don't hide it."

"I've never really been great at being part of a family," she said. "But I sure love yours."

He quirked a smile. "But me best, right? You love me best."

She nodded, glad she could show him her softer side, and her fiery side, and just be herself with him. "I love you best, Dylan."

He swept a kiss along her forehead. "Merry Christmas, sweetheart."

Merry Christmas indeed.

CHAPTER TWENTY-THREE

*D*ylan swung the hammer again and again, sweat dripping from his forehead. So maybe he'd taken on a bigger chunk than he'd known when he'd bought this house.

But hey, the roof was new, and he did have a floor, so Cami couldn't keep teasing him about those things. He had a backyard too—fully fenced once he'd put that in a few months ago—so Athena lived with him now. Had for months, almost when he'd told Cami.

And she couldn't deny that she loved the German shepherd as much as he did. She brought her a ball every other week, and more often than not, it was Cami who took Athena to the park to play.

Of course, Dylan had devoted every waking moment of his life for the past six months to this house. He had floors his feet didn't fall through. And all the rooms framed now. His bedroom was complete, and he'd even allowed Cami to paint it a nice light shade of blue and put in curtains. The kitchen was functional, and so was the bathroom.

Then he'd spent his time on the backyard, the fence, and now he was hammering, hammering, hammering on a new deck while Cami finished a weekend job. Then they were headed over to the downtown park, where the Summerfest was underway. She wanted a churro, and she was convinced they'd find some inspiration for their wedding in the booths that had been set up in the park.

Dylan wanted to do whatever Cami wanted, as he just liked spending time with her, even if it was wandering around a park and buying as many fried foods as they could get.

But he was going to get this deck done first, railings and all. He and Cami had talked about her moving into his place once they were married, and Dylan needed every spare moment between now and September in order to have the house and land ready for her.

"Knock, knock," someone called, and relief ran through him.

"In the back," he called to Pete, wondering how many cowboys he'd roped into coming to help Dylan get the deck done and the rest of the floor laid in the living area.

So maybe Dylan was desperate, and maybe he'd complained a little to Pete about the house.

"Oh, you're making good progress," Pete said when he arrived. "I brought a few people."

Five more men came out onto the small patch of deck Dylan had managed to erect, and he almost started crying.

"Thanks for coming, guys," he said. "I don't have enough hammers for everyone."

"Oh, I saw the flooring in the house," Squire Ackerman said. "I'm going to do that. Your air conditioning works great." He grinned, and Dylan chuckled along with the other guys.

"I'll work out here," Cal said, while Garth and Ethan agreed to help Squire in the house.

Boone said, "I'll stay out here. I don't even know if I know how to hammer something in."

Dylan scoffed. "I know you don't." He grinned at his best friend.

"I can swing a hammer," Pete said. "I did build my own homestead, remember?"

"Oh, we all remember," Squire said. "Too bad Brett's not here. He'd whip us all into shape."

A moment of silence passed, and then someone else called from inside the house. A female voice.

"It's my mom," Squire said. "She brought reinforcements."

Everyone went inside, including Dylan, where Heidi Ackerman, who owned the bakery in Three Rivers, set an overly large box on his kitchen counter.

"Ma." Squire hugged her and swept a kiss across her forehead. "Thanks for bringing food. I don't think Dylan even thought of it."

"I have food," Dylan said, but when Pete opened the box, Dylan realized that he actually didn't have anything edible in his house, not when compared to the doughnuts and muffins now sitting on his countertop.

"Thank you, Heidi," he said, giving the woman a quick hug too. If there was anyone who rivaled his mother in her baking abilities, it was Heidi Ackerman. "Will any of this be at the wedding?"

"Oh, Cami would kill me if I served bear claws at her wedding." She swatted at Dylan. "No, we're having chocolate pudding cake. Cami came in and ordered it last week."

"That's great," he said. "I can't believe she didn't invite me along." Especially for the food visits.

"She's busy," Heidi said.

"Well, maybe you'll make me one to sample." Dylan flashed her his best smile and stepped over to the fridge to pull out a gallon of milk.

They ate, and then the work commenced. He chatted with Pete and Cal, who mercifully didn't quiz him about anything to do with the wedding. Every time he went to his parents' house, it was all anyone could talk about. Cami had to talk about it, though she did try to bring up other things, he knew.

A few hours later, Dylan hammered in the last nail and said, "Well, I think that's it."

"If you want help staining it, let me know," Pete said. "We can get another crew out here."

"Easy," Cal said. "We had to turn boys away from coming today."

"Really?" Dylan asked.

"Yeah," he said. "When there's pay and doughnuts, everyone volunteers." He took off his cowboy hat and wiped his forehead. "Good to see you, Dylan." He shook his hand.

"Bri wants you to come get her every Tuesday and Thursday from now on."

"Is that okay with you?" he asked.

"Sure is. She needs to get out of the house every chance she has."

Dylan followed them inside, pausing to look back over the deck. Yes, this house and yard was going to be exactly what he'd envisioned it to be.

He turned and took a few steps into the kitchen before he realized the rest of the house was now done. "Oh, wow," he said. "This is amazing." And it would've taken him days to lay this floor by himself.

"Thank you," he said. "You guys, thank you so much." Now he could bring in the couches and rugs he'd bought months ago and that had taken up all the space in his garage.

And when Cami showed up later, his house would look like exactly that—a house.

∼

"Is she here?" Dylan asked Boone, who's guest bedroom he currently stood in.

"Yes, she's been here for a while." Boone handed him his bow tie, and Dylan proceeded to put it into position. Cami had shown up. That was good.

Not that Dylan was doubting her. He'd just never envisioned himself as the marrying type—until her.

"Thanks for letting us use your yard," he said to Boone. "Nicole really is a master gardener."

"She'd said September would be the best month," Boone

said. "And she was right. It's like Eden out there." Boone handed him a pair of cufflinks that belonged to Dylan's dad.

Finally, Dylan felt like all the pieces were in place, and now he just had minutes to count down. Boone took him down the hall and through the kitchen, then into the backyard.

Dylan paused to take it all in. This would be everything Cami wanted, and all he could do was hope and pray that *he* could be everything Cami wanted.

He drew in a deep breath and went with Nicole as she escorted him to the altar in the shade. Pastor Scott already stood there, and it seemed everyone who'd been invited had already arrived and taken their seats too.

He hugged his mother and father, each of his sisters, and beamed at his cowboy friends from the ranch. Asher was there with his wife, and so were Dana and Abraham Rogers.

Cami's parents and brother had come from Amarillo, and Dylan had spent a few evenings with them in the days leading up to the wedding. Now, only her mom sat in the first row, a few empty seats saved beside her.

Now all he needed was his bride.

Finally, something seemed to be happening at the end of the aisle opposite of him, and her very small wedding party appeared.

It was Athena, wearing a veil that had a band that went down around her neck. She sat at the end of the aisle, her tongue lolling out of her mouth and the crowd chuckled at her.

Behind her, Cami clutched her father's arm and wore a

beautiful, frilly white dress and a smile as wide as the state of Texas.

Dylan could barely breathe as she took one agonizing step at a time toward him.

"You're beautiful," he whispered as her father passed her to him, and he leaned down to kiss her cheek.

They faced the pastor together, hopefully how they'd face everything in their lives—together.

Dylan squeezed her hand, his nerves on overdrive. Then Pastor Scott started talking, and it was like every Sabbath Day. Dylan's troubles melted away, and when it was time for him to say "I do," he did in a loud, clear voice.

"You may kiss your bride," Pastor Scott said, and Dylan turned toward Cami, grinning like a fool.

"I love you," he said, barely giving her enough time to return the sentiment before he tipped her back and kissed his wife for the first time.

Cheers and yeehaws went up from the crowd, and Dylan couldn't help feeling like the luckiest man in the whole world.

∽

Yay! Dylan and Cami made things work, even when they got tough. **Leave a review now!**

Join Liz's List and never miss a new release or a special sale on her books.

Read on for a sneak peek at **HER COWBOY**

BILLIONAIRE BEST FRIEND, featuring more Christmas romance, this time in Wyoming.

And keep reading after that for a sneak peek of **CHEERING THE COWBOY**, holiday romance at another ranch in Texas.

The End

SNEAK PEEK! HER COWBOY BILLIONAIRE BEST FRIEND CHAPTER ONE

Graham Whittaker gazed at the Tetons, wishing just the tops of the mountains were snow-covered. Unfortunately, it hadn't stopped snowing for a few days, and the white stuff covered everything from the mountaintops to the grass outside the lodge he'd just bought and moved into over Christmas.

He liked to think heaven was weeping for the loss of his father, the same way the Whittaker family had been for the past nine days. With the funeral and burial two days past now, everyone had gone back to their normal lives—except Graham.

"This is your normal life now," he told himself as he turned away from what some probably considered a picturesque view of the country, the snow, the mountains.

Whiskey Mountain Lodge was a beautiful spot, nestled right up against the mountains on the west and the Teton

National park on the north. It had a dozen guest rooms and boasted all the amenities needed to keep them fed, entertained, and happy for days on end.

Not that it mattered. Graham wasn't planning on running the lodge as the quaint bed and breakfast in the mountains that it had previously been.

No, Whiskey Mountain Lodge was his new home.

His father had left behind an entire business that needed running, and Graham had nothing left for him in Seattle anyway. So he'd come to help his mother after the sudden death of her husband, and he'd had enough time to find somewhere to live and operate Springside Energy Operations as the CEO.

It was a step up, really. He'd only been the lead developer at Qualetics Robotics in Seattle, but the itch to develop technology and robotics to make people's lives easier had died when his father had.

Graham hoped it would come back; Springside could definitely benefit from having the first fracking robot to identify the natural gases under the surface of the Earth *before* they drilled. But they were years away from that.

Just like Graham felt years away from anyone else out here.

A dog barked, reminding him that he'd inherited his father's dog as well as his company, and he went over to the back door to let Bear back in. The big black lab seemed to move quite slowly, though he still wore his usual smile on his face.

"Hey, Bear." He scrubbed the dog to wipe off the

snowflakes that had settled on his back. "Guess I better go check on the horses."

Whiskey Mountain had come with a riding stable, something tourists apparently liked to do in the summer months in Wyoming. Graham had grown up in Coral Canyon, Wyoming, but his parents lived in town, in a normal house, without any horses.

Of course, every man in Wyoming learned to ride, and Graham and his three brothers were no exception. But it had been a very, very long time since he'd saddled up in any sense of the word.

But today, though the lodge was a huge building, with dozens of places to which he could escape, he felt trapped. So he plucked his hat from the peg by the door and positioned it on his head. He didn't get many opportunities to wear a cowboy hat in Seattle, but here, he'd worn it every day. And he liked it.

The brim kept the snow off his face as he trudged down the path he'd shoveled every day since moving in and headed toward the stables.

The stables were named DJ Riders, and Graham had no idea where it had come from. There were only three horses that had come with the property, and thankfully, the loft held enough hay to keep them fed for a while.

Graham went through the motions of feeding them, cleaning out their stalls, and making sure they had fresh water that hadn't frozen over. January in Wyoming wasn't for the weak-hearted, that was for sure, horse or human.

The chores done, Graham closed up the stables but turned

away from the lodge up the lane. He had plenty of unpacking to do and no inclination to do it. Besides, it would keep, as he'd been living in the lodge for three days without the family pictures, all the dishes, or more than one towel. He'd survived so far, thanks to a four-wheel-drive vehicle and a pocketful of cash.

He wandered away from the stables, the barn, the rest of the outbuildings of the lodge. He passed a gazebo he hadn't even known existed until that very moment, and he wondered what else he'd find on this parcel of land he'd put his name on. And who knew what spring would bring?

Probably pollen and allergies, he thought, still not entirely happy to be back in Coral Canyon though he'd made the decision to leave his job in Seattle and settle back in his hometown.

The snow muted his footsteps and made it difficult to go very far very fast. Didn't matter. He had the whole day to do whatever he wanted. Tomorrow too. It wasn't until Monday that he'd have to put on a suit and start figuring out how to manage an energy company with over two hundred employees.

He approached another building, this one a bit different than the ones he'd seen before. He wasn't sure what it was, though it looked like a small cabin, with a stovepipe sticking out of the shingles on the roof. Did the lodge have a smaller place to live? Was this another guest area he could rent out?

He stepped closer and peered in the window, not seeing a door anywhere. The place was simply furnished and appeared to be one room with a door leading out of it on his right and into what he assumed was a bedroom.

A woman came out of the bedroom, buttoning her coat.

Graham yelped and backed up at the same time a dog put his front paws on the windowsill inside the house and started barking. And barking. And barking.

With his heart pounding and his adrenaline spiking out of control, Graham's brain didn't seem to be working properly. Therefore, he couldn't move. Didn't even think to move.

So he was still standing there like a peeping Tom when the woman lifted the window and said, "What are you doing here?" in a tone of voice that could've frozen the water into snow if the temperature hadn't already done it.

"I—I—" Graham stammered. "Who are you?"

She cocked her hip, and Graham noticed the long, honey-blonde hair as she threw it over her shoulder before folding her arms. She possessed a pretty face, with a sprinkling of freckles across her cheeks and nose. Her eyes could've been any color, as he was looking from the outside in and the light wasn't the same.

If he'd had to, he'd categorize them as dangerous, especially when they flashed lightning at him.

"I am the owner of this property," she said. "And you're trespassing."

Graham frowned, but at least his brain had started operating normally again. It was his pulse that was galloping now, wondering what he had to do to get invited in to find out what color those eyes were.

"Oh," he said. "I'm sorry. I thought this was my place. I just bought Whiskey Mountain Lodge." He waved in the general direction of the lodge, hoping it was the right way.

"The border is back there about a hundred yards," she

said, still positioned like he might come at her through the window screen. "There's a fence."

"Maybe it's buried in all the snow." Because he had definitely not crossed a fence line. He might have become a city slicker but he still knew what a fence meant. "I'm Graham Whittaker."

A noise halfway between a squeak and a meow came from her mouth. Those eyes rounded, but he still couldn't tell what color they were. "Graham Whittaker?"

He tilted his head now, studying her. Because she knew him. No one spoke with that much surprise in their voice if they didn't know a person.

"Yes," he said slowly. "I'm...." He didn't know how to finish. Everyone in Coral Canyon knew his father had died. Everyone knew the Whittakers had come to mourn. He supposed everyone though they'd all left again, except for his mother and his youngest brother, Beau, who lived in town and worked as a lawyer.

But he didn't know what he was still doing in Coral Canyon, or why he felt the urge to explain it to this woman.

"Just a second." She slammed the window shut and moved away. Feeling stupid, Graham stood there in the snow, wondering what she was going to do. Half a minute later, the dog that had tried to rip his face off through the glass came bounding through the snow from the front of the house.

"Clearwater," the woman called after him, but the dog was either disobedient or didn't care. The blue heeler came right up to Graham and started sniffing him.

Graham chuckled and scratched the dog behind his ears.

"Yeah, I've got a lab. You can probably smell 'im. Bear? His name's Bear."

The blonde woman came around the corner of the cabin, and she stopped much further away than her dog had. "Graham Whittaker." This time she didn't phrase it as a question, and a hint of a smile touched her lips. "You don't remember me, do you?"

Graham abandoned his administrations to the dog and took a step toward her, trying to place her. He thought he'd definitely remember someone as shapely as her, what with those long legs that curved into hips and narrowed to a waist, even in the black jacket she'd buttoned around herself.

He was about to apologize when the answer hit him full in the chest. "Laney Boyd?" He tore his eyes from hers to glance around the land, not that he could tell anything with the piles and piles of snow.

"Is this Echo Ridge Ranch?" he asked. He hadn't realized the lodge property butted up against the ranch where he'd spent time as a teenager. And without looking back at Laney, he knew he'd find a pair of light green eyes. Eyes that came to life when she was atop a horse. Eyes that had always called to him. Eyes that saw more than he'd ever wanted her to. Beautiful, light green eyes he wanted to get to experience again.

When he looked at her again, her grin had filled her whole face. "It's Laney McAllister now," she said, dashing every hope he had of rekindling an old friendship—and maybe making it into something more.

Which is stupid, he told himself as he chuckled and walked through the snow to give her a hug hello. *You just got your heart broken. No need to do it again.*

~

Spend all your Christmases with the Whittaker brothers!
Read HER COWBOY BILLIONAIRE BEST FRIEND now. Available in Kindle Unlimited.

SNEAK PEEK! CHEERING THE COWBOY CHAPTER ONE

*A*ustin Royal washed his hands with the best mechanic's soap available, but the faint black lines of grease never really left his skin. It would have to be enough. He was already late, and there was nothing that made him jumpier than walking into church after the sermon had started. Something his parents had engrained in him since he was a boy.

He took a few precious seconds to smooth his beard, thinking it had come in quite nicely despite what his brothers said. Then he swiped his cowboy hat from the dresser in his bedroom and headed downstairs.

He shared the homestead with his oldest brother, Shane, and his wife, Robin. They'd been married for about three months now, and everyone had worked out a system to keep from stepping on each other's toes.

Dylan had taken over Robin's tiny house, a two hundred

and eight square foot home that she'd parked way down on the end of Cabin Row, where Dylan spent most of his time anyway. He'd built one new cabin already, and had the skeleton of another going up. He worked with the cattle on the ranch the brothers had bought six months ago, and he was halfway through remodeling the home Austin would eventually move into.

Austin grabbed his keys from the hook by the door in the kitchen. "Goin' to church," he called, not really sure where everyone else was at the moment. Someone yelled back to him, and he skipped down the few steps in the garage to one of the trucks they owned.

He was happier than he'd ever been since being forced to leave his family's ranch just outside of San Antonio. He'd just celebrated his thirty-third birthday. By all accounts, Austin should be laughing while he counted his blessings.

But a vein of anger existed in him he didn't know how to deal with. Always there, always just seething right below the surface, the negativity felt like a black plague on his soul. He'd been trying to get to church every week, and sometimes that helped. But he was starting to suspect that it wasn't enough, that nothing would able be able to cure him from this darkness he felt inside himself.

He kept the music off as he drove, using the thirty-minute drive to mentally run through his upcoming week. He craved this solitude, as he'd been working with the three ranch hands that had come with Triple Towers when he and his brothers had bought it.

Oaker and Carlos were friendly enough. They'd educated

all the brothers about where things were and how things were done. Shane had changed almost all of it, because the ranch was in complete disrepair, both physically and financially.

Dylan had taken care of the outbuildings. Together, he and Shane were working on the pasture rotations, getting more hay planted, and dealing with all the legal rights with the water on the ranch. Austin had been tasked with all the horse care—which wasn't much, considering they had four horses.

Shane had brought one over from Grape Seed Ranch, where the brothers used to work, and Dylan and his fiancée, Hazel, and Austin had purchased a horse each from Levi Rhodes. Austin loved horses and didn't mind the time it took to care for them. Robin, who was a professional farrier, did quite a bit to keep them shod and healthy too.

Austin's real love, surprisingly, came with the huge hen house that had come with the ranch. Shane had wanted to sell the chickens and knock down the coop in favor of something else. But Austin had taken a liking to the clucking, the methodical gathering of eggs, and the seemingly constant need to feed the beasts.

With one hundred and four chickens to care for, Austin spent a lot of time in that coop. It had become his sanctuary of sorts, and he wasn't sure if he should chuckle at that or take the fact of the matter to his grave.

When he wasn't doing those tasks, he worked with Shayleigh in the equipment shed, thus the grease stains in his fingerprints. She'd been an Army mechanic, and while she was as beautiful as an angel, she had the disposition of a cornered wildcat.

He got along best with her out of anyone, so he'd been enduring hours with her in the afternoon, under her rough hand of correction, his patience thinning by the day. She went to the same church as him, but he deliberately didn't ask her to drive in with him, nor did he sit by her. He'd asked—once.

The look of disdain she'd given him had been scathing enough to remind him each week that she was not interested. Fine by him. He needed the thirty minutes in and the thirty minutes back to re-center himself anyway. And her presence was anything but centering.

He arrived in plenty of time to park where he wanted and sit on the far right side the way he liked. Sometimes a couple of cowboys he knew from other ranches and farms surrounding the town of Grape Seed Falls sat by him, but today, the crowd was thin.

Didn't matter. Austin needed to be there, even if it was just him and the minister.

Pastor Gifford got up and said, "Everyone must be home baking pies today," and Austin remembered that it was nearly Thanksgiving. His mother would be joining them on the ranch on the Wednesday before the holiday, and he'd be the one to make sure she got settled. He always was, though Dylan and Shane took care of their mom too.

The pastor spoke about being grateful, accepting help when it was offered, and offering service at this time of year to those who might need it. "Pray for opportunities to serve others," he said. "The Lord can use you. He will use you."

Austin felt like he could barely keep his head above water most days. He didn't get a chance to interact with many people outside the ranch, but he supposed there were still plenty of opportunities to help the ranch hands or his brothers with something. Wasn't there?

After the service ended, Austin stayed in his seat while everyone else filed out. Pastor Gifford would be busy for several minutes, and Austin needed a few minutes before their meeting anyway.

He'd finally plucked up the courage to ask Pastor Gifford for help. Was that why the minister had focused his speech today about accepting help or looking for ways to serve? What if that was all Austin needed to hear?

He closed his eyes and prayed, asking God for guidance, for a way to cleanse himself from his dark thoughts. No definitive answer came, not that Austin was expecting it to.

When there was little noise left coming from the foyer, Austin stood and made his way there. Pastor Gifford saw him and finished saying good-bye to the last couple. "Austin," he said warmly, a smile on his face that felt one-hundred percent genuine. "Let's go talk in my office."

He led the way down a short hall and around the corner before pushing through a thick door and into a decent-sized office. He pulled his tie loose around his neck and sighed as he sat.

"What can I help you with today?" He folded his arms on his desk and looked at Austin expectantly.

Austin removed his cowboy hat and worried his fingers along the brim. He sat too, wishing the words would magically align themselves. "Well, I'm not really sure...."

"What's bothering you?"

Austin looked at the man, probably close to his father's age. The thought of his father clarified things. "I'm angry," he said. "About a lot of things that shouldn't make me angry. I don't feel...normal. It's always there, and I don't know how to get rid of it."

Pastor Gifford nodded. "Go on."

"I think...I just need to know what to do."

The minister shook his head, though a smaller version of the smile he'd worn in the foyer returned. "I can't tell you what to do." He opened a desk drawer and turned his attention to that. "Let me see...I think I have something you might try."

Austin wanted a pill, maybe some magic beans, anything that would take this feeling away. He leaned forward as Pastor Gifford placed a simple business card on the desk.

"Anger management?" Austin read the card. "Classes, meetings, and more. Thursdays at seven p.m." He looked at the pastor. "You think I should go to anger management classes?"

"I've had several patrons who've attended," he said, nudging the card closer. "They speak highly of the program."

Austin took the card, but it felt too heavy to take home with him. "All right. Thanks." He stood, disappointed, not quite expecting the minister to give him more to do. That well of anger he barely kept contained started boiling, and Austin needed to leave. Now.

He stuffed the card in his back pocket and left the office, then the church. The wind tried to steal his hat from right off the top of his head—another thing to make him angry. The blasted wind. Who got angry over wind?

∼

Time seemed to move slowly, but Thursday eventually came. He didn't want to tell anyone where he was going, because then they'd want to know why. And he didn't want Shane or Dylan to A. worry, or B. ask him questions, or C. give him advice.

Sure, he knew Shane spoke with a therapist regularly, using an app called Talk To Me. It had done amazing things for Shane's own pent-up anger and feelings of abandonment. Dylan didn't seem to have quite as many problems, but Austin had noticed that he'd stopped talking to their father about a year ago. He seemed happier for it too, and Hazel had really helped in that department as well.

Austin, the youngest, still unattached, was lonely. Angry about being lonely. Sad. Angry about being sad. And most of all, he was completely done with being duped by his dad. That was what made him the angriest, and he decided while he put his horse away on Thursday evening that he would go to the anger management meeting.

He met Robin on his way out of the stable, and seized the opportunity. "Hey, I'm heading into town tonight. Can you tell Shane?"

"Sure." She didn't give him a funny look or question why he'd go into town on a Thursday. Now if he could just get the keys and get out of there....

He managed to do both without seeing anyone except

Shay, who had her two German shepherds engaged in some sort of training exercise. Her dogs were beautiful and well-behaved, and she spent serious time making sure of both.

It was barely five-thirty when he arrived in Grape Seed Falls, so Austin bummed around town, got dinner, and finally parked at the library a few minutes before the meeting was set to start. Maybe he could sneak in the back and just listen.

With only two minutes to spare, he got out of the truck and went inside the lower level of the library, where all the meeting rooms were located. Low-level chatter met his ears from a room at the end of the hall, and he slicked his palms down the front of his jeans.

His heart pounded, and he felt like he was walking the plank, heading right for a watery grave. The door stood open and a patch of brighter light fell onto the carpet. The scent of chocolate and something fruity met his nose, but it wasn't comforting the way it had been when his mother had baked cookies for the boys after school.

He paused a few strides away from the door, his mind still warring with itself. He hadn't seen anyone yet, and he could just walk on by. Pretend he'd come to the wrong room. Anything. Something.

Just go inside.

The words entered his mind, erasing and silencing the jumbled mess his thoughts had become.

So he straightened his shoulders and marched toward the room, deciding once and for all that he was not going to let his anger rule his life. Not anymore.

His first step in the room and someone moved right in

front of him. He couldn't slow. Couldn't stop. Couldn't dodge.

His instinct kicked in and he had a half-second to brace before he collided with another body. A softer body than his, but still hard in specific places. He grabbed onto her arms—it was a woman with streaked hair. Pink tips.

Something cold and wet seeped through his shirt, and he looked down at his chest.

Punch. Red punch.

"Let go of me." The woman spoke in a near-growl, and Austin hastened to obey her, unsure of when he'd clamped his fingers around her biceps.

Another step back, and all his senses started working again. Eyes. Nose. Ears.

A hush had fallen on the room, and he glanced around to find at least a dozen people in attendance, including the woman he'd barreled straight into

"Shay?" he asked.

She accepted a handful of napkins from another woman and started mopping up her own ruined shirt. She wore a pair of jeans that hugged every feminine curve, the same pair of cowgirl boots he'd seen countless times, and a pretty sea foam green shirt. Well, it used to be pretty. Now with the red stain, it looked like a Christmas nightmare.

"What are you doin' here?" she asked, and not kindly. Her hazel eyes flashed with annoyance, but she didn't look fully at him until she'd thrown away the wad of napkins.

She folded her arms and cocked her hip, and Austin should not have found her so attractive. After all, this was going to be an argument, and he wouldn't walk away the winner. He rarely did with Shayleigh Hatch.

But she was gorgeous, and strong, and feminine all at the same time. He'd sensed a softer Shay under the hard armor she presented to the world, but he hadn't cracked it. Hadn't even tried. Wasn't sure it was worth the effort.

But now, staring at her in this new environment where she couldn't boss him around and couldn't make him feel two inches tall, Austin wondered if the spark he'd always felt between them was really as one-sided as she'd claimed it to be.

So he'd asked her to dance at his brother's wedding. He could admit it. She'd turned him down by laughing in his face and saying she'd never be interested in him. His place with her had been made very clear, and he hadn't tried to move from the corner she'd put him in.

But now…. Now something started to buzz in his bloodstream. Whisper fantasies through his mind. Fan that dormant flame into something brilliant and hot.

"Let it go, Shay," the woman who'd brought her the napkins said, stepping between her and Austin. "It's time to start." She cast a nervous look at Austin that said, *Please just go sit down. Or leave. Something.*

Shay drew in a deep breath through her nose, her glare miraculously dropping in intensity. "Time to start. Right."

She turned away from him, and then twisted back to say, "I think the meeting for men who steal women's ranches is upstairs," in a cold, dismissive tone that made all the parts of Austin that had started to hum quiet.

Especially when Shay rounded the few rows of chairs that

had been set up, took her position at the front of the room, and said, "All right, everyone. Welcome to our weekly meeting. It's time to begin."

∽

Read CHEERING THE COWBOY now. Available in Kindle Unlimited.

BOOKS IN THE CHRISTMAS IN CORAL CANYON ROMANCE SERIES

Her Cowboy Billionaire Best Friend (Book 1): Graham Whittaker returns to Coral Canyon a few days after Christmas—after the death of his father. He takes over the energy company his dad built from the ground up and buys a high-end lodge to live in—only a mile from the home of his once-best friend, Laney McAllister. They were best friends once, but Laney's always entertained feelings for him, and spending so much time with him while they make Christmas memories puts her heart in danger of getting broken again...

Her Cowboy Billionaire Boss (Book 2): Since the death of his wife a few years ago, Eli Whittaker has been running from one job to another, unable to find somewhere for him and his son to settle. Meg Palmer is Stockton's nanny, and she comes with her boss, Eli, to the lodge, her long-time crush on the man no different in Wyoming than it was on the beach. When she confesses her feelings for him and gets nothing in return, she's crushed, embarrassed, and unsure if she can stay in Coral Canyon for Christmas. Then Eli starts to show some feelings for her too...

Her Cowboy Billionaire Boyfriend (Book 3): Andrew Whittaker is the public face for the Whittaker Brothers' family energy company, and with his older brother's robot about to be announced, he needs a press secretary to help him get everything ready and tour the state to make the announcements. When he's hit by a protest sign being carried by the company's biggest opponent, Rebecca Collings, he learns with a few clicks that she has the background they need. He offers her the job of press secretary when she thought she was going to be arrested, and not only because the spark between them in so hot Andrew can't see straight.

Can Becca and Andrew work together and keep their relationship a secret? Or will hearts break in this classic romance retelling reminiscent of *Two Weeks Notice*?

Her Cowboy Billionaire Bodyguard (Book 4): Beau Whittaker has watched his brothers find love one by one, but every attempt he's made has ended in disaster. Lily Everett has been in the spotlight since childhood and has half a dozen platinum records with her two sisters. She's taking a break from the brutal music industry and hiding out in Wyoming while her ex-husband continues to cause trouble for her. When she hears of Beau Whittaker and what he offers his clients, she wants to meet him. Beau is instantly attracted to Lily, but he tried a relationship with his last client that left a scar that still hasn't healed...

Can Lily use the spirit of Christmas to discover what matters most? Will Beau open his heart to the possibility of love with someone so different from him?

BOOKS IN THE GRAPE SEED FALLS ROMANCE SERIES:

Choosing the Cowboy (Book 1): With financial trouble and personal issues around every corner, can Maggie Duffin and Chase Carver rely on their faith to find their happily-ever-after?

A spinoff from the #1 bestselling Three Rivers Ranch Romance novels, also by USA Today bestselling author Liz Isaacson.

Craving the Cowboy (Book 2): Dwayne Carver is set to inherit his family's ranch in the heart of Texas Hill Country, and in order to keep up with his ranch duties and fulfill his dreams of owning a horse farm, he hires top trainer Felicity Lightburne. They get along great, and she can envision herself on this new farm—at least until her mother falls ill and she has to return to help her. Can Dwayne and Felicity work through their differences to find their happily-ever-after?

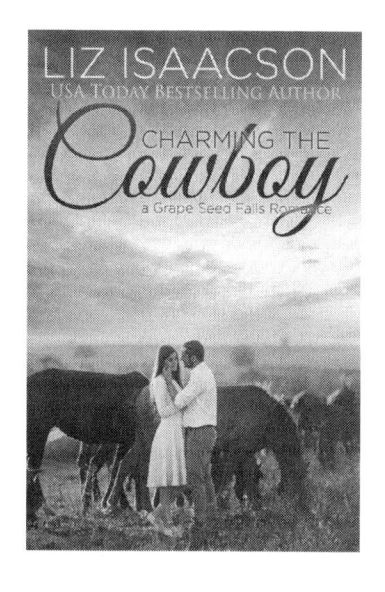

Charming the Cowboy (Book 3): Third grade teacher Heather Carver has had her eye on Levi Rhodes for a couple of years now, but he seems to be blind to her attempts to charm him. When she breaks her arm while on his horse ranch, Heather infiltrates Levi's life in ways he's never thought of, and his strict anti-female stance slips. Will Heather heal his emotional scars and he care for her physical ones so they can have a real relationship?

Courting the Cowboy (Book 4): Frustrated with the cowboy-only dating scene in Grape Seed Falls, May Sotheby joins TexasFaithful.com, hoping to find her soul mate without having to relocate--or deal with cowboy hats and boots. She has no idea that Kurt Pemberton, foreman at Grape Seed Ranch, is the man she starts communicating with... Will May be able to follow her heart and get Kurt to forgive her so they can be together?

Claiming the Cowboy, Royal Brothers Book 1 (Grape Seed Falls Romance Book 5): Unwilling to be tied down, farrier Robin Cook has managed to pack her entire life into a two-hundred-and-eighty square-foot house, and that includes her Yorkie. Cowboy and co-foreman, Shane Royal has had his heart set on Robin for three years, even though she flat-out turned him down the last time he asked her to dinner. But she's back at Grape Seed Ranch for five weeks as she works her horseshoeing magic, and he's still interested, despite a bitter life lesson that left a bad taste for marriage in his mouth.

Robin's interested in him too. But can she find room for Shane in her tiny house--and can he take a chance on her with his tired heart?

Catching the Cowboy, Royal Brothers Book 2 (Grape Seed Falls Romance Book 6): Dylan Royal is good at two things: whistling and caring for cattle. When his cows are being attacked by an unknown wild animal, he calls Texas Parks & Wildlife for help. He wasn't expecting a beautiful mammologist to show up, all flirty and fun and everything Dylan didn't know he wanted in his life.

Hazel Brewster has gone on more first dates than anyone in Grape Seed Falls, and she thinks maybe Dylan deserves a second... Can they find their way through wild animals, huge life changes, and their emotional pasts to find their forever future?

Cheering the Cowboy, Royal Brothers Book 3 (Grape Seed Falls Romance Book 7): Austin Royal loves his life on his new ranch with his brothers. But he doesn't love that Shayleigh Hatch came with the property, nor that he has to take the blame for the fact that he now owns her childhood ranch. They rarely have a conversation that doesn't leave him furious and frustrated--and yet he's still attracted to Shay in a strange, new way.

Shay inexplicably likes him too, which utterly confuses and angers her. As they work to make this Christmas the best the Triple Towers Ranch has ever seen, can they also navigate through their rocky relationship to smoother waters?

BOOKS IN THE STEEPLE RIDGE ROMANCE SERIES:

Starting Over at Steeple Ridge: Steeple Ridge Romance (Book 1): Tucker Jenkins has had enough of tall buildings, traffic, and has traded in his technology firm in New York City for Steeple Ridge Horse Farm in rural Vermont. Missy Marino has worked at the farm since she was a teen, and she's always dreamed of owning it. But her ex-husband left her with a truckload of debt, making her fantasies of owning the farm unfulfilled. Tucker didn't come to the country to find a new wife, but he supposes a woman could help him start over in Steeple Ridge. Will Tucker and Missy be able to navigate the shaky ground between them to find a new beginning?

Finding Love at Steeple Ridge: A Butters Brothers Novel, Steeple Ridge Romance (Book 2): Ben Buttars is the youngest of the four Buttars brothers who come to Steeple Ridge Farm, and he finally feels like he's landed somewhere he can make a life for himself. Reagan Cantwell is a decade older than Ben and the recreational direction for the town of Island Park. Though Ben is young, he knows what he wants—and that's Rae. Can she figure out how to put what matters most in her life—family and faith—above her job before she loses Ben?

Learning Faith at Steeple Ridge: A Butters Brothers Novel, Steeple Ridge Romance (Book 3): Sam Buttars has spent the last decade making sure he and his brothers stay together. They've been at Steeple Ridge for a while now, but with the youngest married and happy, the siren's call to return to his parents' farm in Wyoming is loud in Sam's ears. He'd just go if it weren't for beautiful Bonnie Sherman, who roped his heart the first time he saw her. Do Sam and Bonnie have the faith to find comfort in each other instead of in the people who've already passed?

Learning Faith at Steeple Ridge: A Butters Brothers Novel, Steeple Ridge Romance (Book 4): Logan Buttars has always been good-natured and happy-go-lucky. After watching two of his brothers settle down, he recognizes a void in his life he didn't know about. Veterinarian Layla Guyman has appreciated Logan's friendship and easy way with animals when he comes into the clinic to get the service dogs. But with his future at Steeple Ridge in the balance, she's not sure a relationship with him is worth the risk. Can she rely on her faith and employ patience to tame Logan's wild heart?

Learning Faith at Steeple Ridge: A Butters Brothers Novel, Steeple Ridge Romance (Book 5): Darren Buttars is cool, collected, and quiet—and utterly devastated when his girlfriend of nine months, Farrah Irvine, breaks up with him because he wanted her to ride her horse in a parade. But Farrah doesn't ride anymore, a fact she made very clear to Darren. She returned to her childhood home with so much baggage, she doesn't know where to start with the unpacking. Darren's the only Buttars brother who isn't married, and he wants to make Island Park his permanent home—with Farrah. Can they find their way through the heartache to achieve a happily-ever-after together?

BOOKS IN THE GOLD VALLEY ROMANCE SERIES:

Before the Leap: A Gold Valley Romance (Book 1): Jace Lovell only has one thing left after his fiancé abandons him at the altar: his job at Horseshoe Home Ranch. Belle Edmunds is back in Gold Valley and she's desperate to build a portfolio that she can use to start her own firm in Montana. Jace isn't anywhere near forgiving his fiancé, and he's not sure he's ready for a new relationship with someone as fiery and beautiful as Belle. Can she employ her patience while he figures out how to forgive so they can find their own brand of happily-ever-after?

After the Fall: A Gold Valley Romance (Book 2): Professional snowboarder Sterling Maughan has sequestered himself in his family's cabin in the exclusive mountain community above Gold Valley, Montana after a devastating fall that ended his career. Norah Watson cleans Sterling's cabin and the more time they spend together, the more Sterling is interested in all things Norah. As his body heals, so does his faith. Will Norah be able to trust Sterling so they can have a chance at true love?

Through the Mist: A Gold Valley Romance (Book 3): Landon Edmunds has been a cowboy his whole life. An accident five years ago ended his successful rodeo career, and now he's looking to start a horse ranch--and he's looking outside of Montana. Which would be great if God hadn't brought Megan Palmer back to Gold Valley right when Landon is looking to leave. Megan and Landon work together well, and as sparks fly, she's sure God brought her back to Gold Valley so she could find her happily ever after. Through serious discussion and prayer, can Landon and Megan find their future together?

Be sure to check out the spinoff series, the Brush Creek Brides romances after you read THROUGH THE MIST. Start with A WEDDING FOR THE WIDOWER.

Between the Reins: A Gold Valley Romance (Book 4): Twelve years ago, Owen Carr left Gold Valley—and his long-time girlfriend—in favor of a country music career in Nashville. Married and divorced, Natalie teaches ballet at the dance studio in Gold Valley, but she never auditioned for the professional company the way she dreamed of doing. With Owen back, she realizes all the opportunities she missed out on when he left all those years ago—including a future with him. Can they mend broken bridges in order to have a second chance at love?

Over the Moon: A Gold Valley Romance (Book 5): Caleb Chamberlain has spent the last five years recovering from a horrible breakup, his alcoholism that stemmed from it, and the car accident that left him hospitalized. He's finally on the right track in his life—until Holly Gray, his twin brother's ex-fiance mistakes him for Nathan. Holly's back in Gold Valley to get the required veterinarian hours to apply for her graduate program. When the herd at Horseshoe Home comes down with pneumonia, Caleb and Holly are forced to work together in close quarters. Holly's over Nathan, but she hasn't forgiven him—or the woman she believes broke up their relationship. Can Caleb and Holly navigate such a rough past to find their happily-ever-after?

Journey to Steeple Ridge Farm with Holly—and fall in love with the cowboys there in the Steeple Ridge Romance series! Start with STARTING OVER AT STEEPLE RIDGE.

Under the Bridge: A Gold Valley Romance (Book 6): Ty Barker has been dancing through the last thirty years of his life--and he's suddenly realized he's alone. River Lee Whitely is back in Gold Valley with her two little girls after a divorce that's left deep scars. She has a job at Silver Creek that requires her to be able to ride a horse, and she nearly tramples Ty at her first lesson. That's just fine by him, because River Lee is the girl Ty has never gotten over. Ty realizes River Lee needs time to settle into her new job, her new home, her new life as a single parent, but going slow has never been his style. But for River Lee, can Ty take the necessary steps to keep her in his life?

Up on the Housetop: A Gold Valley Romance (Book 7): Archer Bailey has already lost one job to Emersyn Enders, so he deliberately doesn't tell her about the cowhand job up at Horseshoe Home Ranch. Emery's temporary job is ending, but her obligations to her physically disabled sister aren't. As Archer and Emery work together, its clear that the sparks flying between them aren't all from their friendly competition over a job. Will Emery and Archer be able to navigate the ranch, their close quarters, and their individual circumstances to find love this holiday season?

Around the Bend: A Gold Valley Romance (Book 8): Cowboy Elliott Hawthorne has just lost his best friend and cabin mate to the worst thing imaginable—marriage. When his brother calls about an accident with their father, Elliott rushes down to Gold Valley from the ranch only to be met with the most beautiful woman he's ever seen. His father's new physical therapist, London Marsh, likes the handsome face and gentle spirit she sees in Elliott too. Can Elliott and London navigate difficult family situations to find a happily-ever-after?

Second Chance Ranch: A Three Rivers Ranch Romance (Book 1): After his deployment, injured and discharged Major Squire Ackerman returns to Three Rivers Ranch, wanting to forgive Kelly for ignoring him a decade ago. He'd like to provide the stable life she needs, but with old wounds opening and a ranch on the brink of financial collapse, it will take patience and faith to make their second chance possible.

Third Time's the Charm: A Three Rivers Ranch Romance (Book 2): First Lieutenant Peter Marshall has a truckload of debt and no way to provide for a family, but Chelsea helps him see past all the obstacles, all the scars. With so many unknowns, can Pete and Chelsea develop the love, acceptance, and faith needed to find their happily ever after?

Fourth and Long: A Three Rivers Ranch Romance (Book 3): Commander Brett Murphy goes to Three Rivers Ranch to find some rest and relaxation with his Army buddies. Having his ex-wife show up with a seven-year-old she claims is his son is anything but the R&R he craves. Kate needs to make amends, and Brett needs to find forgiveness, but are they too late to find their happily ever after?

Fifth Generation Cowboy: A Three Rivers Ranch Romance (Book 4): Tom Lovell has watched his friends find their true happiness on Three Rivers Ranch, but everywhere he looks, he only sees friends. Rose Reyes has been bringing her daughter out to the ranch for equine therapy for months, but it doesn't seem to be working. Her challenges with Mari are just as frustrating as ever. Could Tom be exactly what Rose needs? Can he remove his friendship blinders and find love with someone who's been right in front of him all this time?

Sixth Street Love Affair: A Three Rivers Ranch Romance (Book 5): After losing his wife a few years back, Garth Ahlstrom thinks he's ready for a second chance at love. But Juliette Thompson has a secret that could destroy their budding relationship. Can they find the strength, patience, and faith to make things work?

The Seventh Sergeant: A Three Rivers Ranch Romance (Book 6): Life has finally started to settle down for Sergeant Reese Sanders after his devastating injury overseas. Discharged from the Army and now with a good job at Courage Reins, he's finally found happiness—until a horrific fall puts him right back where he was years ago: Injured and depressed. Carly Watters, Reese's new veteran care coordinator, dislikes small towns almost as much as she loathes cowboys. But she finds herself faced with both when she gets assigned to Reese's case. Do they have the humility and faith to make their relationship more than professional?

Eight Second Ride: A Three Rivers Ranch Romance (Book 7): Ethan Greene loves his work at Three Rivers Ranch, but he can't seem to find the right woman to settle down with. When sassy yet vulnerable Brynn Bowman shows up at the ranch to recruit him back to the rodeo circuit, he takes a different approach with the barrel racing champion. His patience and newfound faith pay off when a friendship--and more--starts with Brynn. But she wants out of the rodeo circuit right when Ethan wants to rejoin. Can they find the path God wants them to take and still stay together?

The First Lady of Three Rivers Ranch: A Three Rivers Ranch Romance (Book 8): Heidi Duffin has been dreaming about opening her own bakery since she was thirteen years old. She scrimped and saved for years to afford baking and pastry school in San Francisco. And now she only has one year left before she's a certified pastry chef. Frank Ackerman's father has recently retired, and he's taken over the largest cattle ranch in the Texas Panhandle. A horseman through and through, he's also nearing thirty-one and looking for someone to bring love and joy to a homestead that's been dominated by men for a decade. But when he convinces Heidi to come clean the cowboy cabins, she changes all that. But the siren's call of a bakery is still loud in Heidi's ears, even if she's also seeing a future with Frank. Can she rely on her faith in ways she's never had to before or will their relationship end when summer does?

Christmas in Three Rivers: A Three Rivers Ranch Romance (Book 9): Isn't Christmas the best time to fall in love? The cowboys of Three Rivers Ranch think so. Join four of them as they journey toward their path to happily ever after in four, all-new novellas in the Amazon #1 Bestselling Three Rivers Ranch Romance series.

THE NINTH INNING: The Christmas season has never felt like such a burden to boutique owner Andrea Larsen. But with Mama gone and the holidays upon her, Andy finds herself wishing she hadn't been so quick to judge her former boyfriend, cowboy Lawrence Collins. Well, Lawrence hasn't forgotten about Andy either, and he devises a plan to get her out to the ranch so they can reconnect. Do they have the faith and humility to patch things up and start a new relationship?

TEN DAYS IN TOWN: Sandy Keller is tired of the dating scene in Three Rivers. Though she owns the pancake house, she's looking for a fresh start, which means an escape from the town where she grew up. When her older brother's best friend, Tad Jorgensen, comes to town for the holidays, it is a balm to his weary soul. A helicopter tour guide who experienced a near-death experience, he's looking to start over too--but in Three Rivers. Can Sandy and Tad navigate their troubles to find the path God wants them to take--and discover true love--in only ten days?

ELEVEN YEAR REUNION: Pastry chef extraordinaire, Grace Lewis has moved to Three Rivers to help Heidi Ackerman open a bakery in Three Rivers. Grace relishes the idea of starting over in a town where no one knows about her failed cupcakery. She doesn't expect to run into her old high school boyfriend, Jonathan Carver. A carpenter working at Three Rivers Ranch, Jon's in town against his will. But with Grace now on the scene, Jon's thinking life in Three Rivers is suddenly looking up. But with her focus on baking and his disdain for small towns, can they make their eleven year reunion stick?

THE TWELFTH TOWN: Newscaster Taryn Tucker has had enough of life on-screen. She's bounced from town to town before arriving in Three Rivers, completely alone and completely anonymous--just the way she now likes it. She takes a job cleaning at Three Rivers Ranch, hoping for a chance to figure out who she is and where God wants her. When she meets happy-go-lucky cowhand Kenny Stockton, she doesn't expect sparks to fly. Kenny's always been "the best friend" for his female friends, but the pull between him and Taryn can't be denied. Will they have the courage and faith necessary to make their opposite worlds mesh?

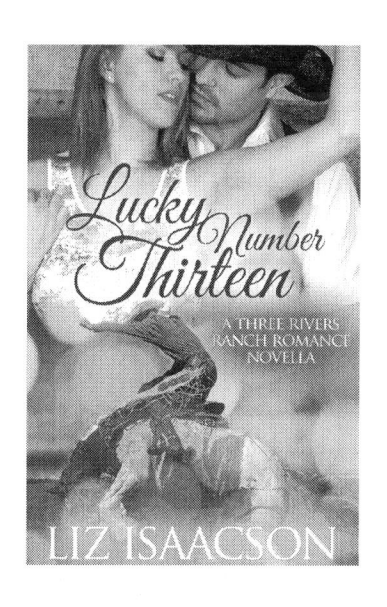

Lucky Number Thirteen: A Three Rivers Ranch Romance (Book 10): Tanner Wolf, a rodeo champion ten times over, is excited to be riding in Three Rivers for the first time since he left his philandering ways and found religion. Seeing his old friends Ethan and Brynn is therapuetic--until a terrible accident lands him in the hospital. With his rodeo career over, Tanner thinks maybe he'll stay in town--and it's not just because his nurse, Summer Hamblin, is the prettiest woman he's ever met. But Summer's the queen of first dates, and as she looks for a way to make a relationship with the transient rodeo star work Summer's not sure she has the fortitude to go on a second date. Can they find love among the tragedy?

The Curse of February Fourteenth: A Three Rivers Ranch Romance (Book 11): Cal Hodgkins, cowboy veterinarian at Bowman's Breeds, isn't planning to meet anyone at the masked dance in small-town Three Rivers. He just wants to get his bachelor friends off his back and sit on the sidelines to drink his punch. But when he sees a woman dressed in gorgeous butterfly wings and cowgirl boots with blue stitching, he's smitten. Too bad she runs away from the dance before he can get her name, leaving only her boot behind...

Fifteen Minutes of Fame: A Three Rivers Ranch Romance (Book 12): Navy Richards is thirty-five years of tired—tired of dating the same men, working a demanding job, and getting her heart broken over and over again. Her aunt has always spoken highly of the matchmaker in Three Rivers, Texas, so she takes a six-month sabbatical from her high-stress job as a pediatric nurse, hops on a bus, and meets with the matchmaker. Then she meets Gavin Redd. He's handsome, he's hardworking, and he's a cowboy. But is he an Aquarius too? Navy's not making a move until she knows for sure...

Sixteen Steps to Fall in Love: A Three Rivers Ranch Romance (Book 13): A chance encounter at a dog park sheds new light on the tall, talented Boone that Nicole can't ignore. As they get to know each other better and start to dig into each other's past, Nicole is the one who wants to run. This time from her growing admiration and attachment to Boone. From her aging parents. From herself.

But Boone feels the attraction between them too, and he decides he's tired of running and ready to make Three Rivers his permanent home. **Can Boone and Nicole use their faith to overcome their differences and find a happily-ever-after together?**

The Sleigh on Seventeenth Street: A Three Rivers Ranch Romance (Book 14): A cowboy with skills as an electrician tries a relationship with a down-on-her luck plumber. Can Dylan and Camila make water and electricity play nicely together this Christmas season? Or will they get shocked as they try to make their relationship work?

BOOKS IN THE BRUSH CREEK BRIDES ROMANCE SERIES:

A Wedding for the Widower: Brush Creek Brides Romance (Book 1): Former rodeo champion and cowboy Walker Thompson trains horses at Brush Creek Horse Ranch, where he lives a simple life in his cabin with his ten-year-old son. A widower of six years, he's worked with Tess Wagner, a widow who came to Brush Creek to escape the turmoil of her life to give her seven-year-old son a slower pace of life. But Tess's breast cancer is back...

Walker will have to decide if he'd rather spend even a short time with Tess than not have her in his life at all. Tess wants to feel God's love and power, but can she discover and accept God's will in order to find her happy ending?

A Companion for the Cowboy: Brush Creek Brides Romance (Book 2): Cowboy and professional roper Justin Jackman has found solitude at Brush Creek Horse Ranch, preferring his time with the animals he trains over dating. With two failed engagements in his past, he's not really interested in getting his heart stomped on again. But when flirty and fun Renee Martin picks him up at a church ice cream bar--on a bet, no less--he finds himself more than just a little interested. His Gen-X attitudes are attractive to her; her Millennial behaviors drive him nuts. Can Justin look past their differences and take a chance on another engagement?

A Bride for the Bronc Rider: Brush Creek Brides Romance (Book 3): Ted Caldwell has been a retired bronc rider for years, and he thought he was perfectly happy training horses to buck at Brush Creek Ranch. He was wrong. When he meets April Nox, who comes to the ranch to hide her pregnancy from all her friends back in Jackson Hole, Ted realizes he has a huge family-shaped hole in his life. April is embarrassed, heartbroken, and trying to find her extinguished faith. She's never ridden a horse and wants nothing to do with a cowboy ever again. Can Ted and April create a family of happiness and love from a tragedy?

A Family for the Farmer: Brush Creek Brides Romance (Book 4): Blake Gibbons oversees all the agriculture at Brush Creek Horse Ranch, sometimes moonlighting as a general contractor. When he meets Erin Shields, new in town, at her aunt's bakery, he's instantly smitten. Erin moved to Brush Creek after a divorce that left her penniless, homeless, and a single mother of three children under age eight. She's nowhere near ready to start dating again, but the longer Blake hangs around the bakery, the more she starts to like him. Can Blake and Erin find a way to blend their lifestyles and become a family?

A Home for the Horseman: Brush Creek Brides Romance (Book 5): Emmett Graves has always had a positive outlook on life. He adores training horses to become barrel racing champions during the day and cuddling with his cat at night. Fresh off her professional rodeo retirement, Molly Brady comes to Brush Creek Horse Ranch as Emmett's protege. He's not thrilled, and she's allergic to cats. Oh, and she'd like to stay cowboy-free, thank you very much. But Emmett's about as cowboy as they come.... Can Emmett and Molly work together without falling in love?

A Refuge for the Rancher: Brush Creek Brides Romance (Book 6): Grant Ford spends his days training cattle—when he's not camped out at the elementary school hoping to catch a glimpse of his ex-girlfriend. When principal Shannon Sharpe confronts him and asks him to stay away from the school, the spark between them is instant and hot. Shannon's expecting a transfer very soon, but she also needs a summer outdoor coordinator—and Grant fits the bill. Just because he's handsome and everything Shannon's ever wanted in a cowboy husband means nothing. Will Grant and Shannon be able to survive the summer or will the Utah heat be too much for them to handle?

A Marriage for the Marine: A Fuller Family Novel - Brush Creek Brides Romance (Book 7): Tate Benson can't believe he's come to Nowhere, Utah, to fix up a house that hasn't been inhabited in years. But he has. Because he's retired from the Marines and looking to start a life as a police officer in small-town Brush Creek. Wren Fuller has her hands full most days running her family's company. When Tate calls and demands a maid for that morning, she decides to have the calls forwarded to her cell and go help him out. She didn't know he was moving in next door, and she's completely unprepared for his handsomeness, his kind heart, and his wounded soul. Can Tate and Wren weather a relationship when they're also next-door neighbors?

A Fiancé for the Firefighter: A Fuller Family Novel - Brush Creek Brides Romance (Book 8): Cora Wesley comes to Brush Creek, hoping to get some in-the-wild firefighting training as she prepares to put in her application to be a hotshot. When she meets Brennan Fuller, the spark between them is hot and instant. As they get to know each other, her deadline is constantly looming over them, and Brennan starts to wonder if he can break ranks in the family business. He's okay mowing lawns and hanging out with his brothers, but he dreams of being able to go to college and become a landscape architect, but he's just not sure it can be done. Will Cora and Brennan be able to endure their trials to find true love?

A Treasure for the Trooper: A Fuller Family Novel - Brush Creek Brides Romance (Book 9): Dawn Fuller has made some mistakes in her life, and she's not proud of the way McDermott Boyd found her off the road one day last year. She's spent a hard year wrestling with her choices and trying to fix them, glad for McDermott's acceptance and friendship. He lost his wife years ago, done his best with his daughter, and now he's ready to move on. Can McDermott help Dawn find a way past her former mistakes and down a path that leads to love, family, and happiness?

A Date for the Detective: A Fuller Family Novel - Brush Creek Brides Romance (Book 10): Dahlia Reid is one of the best detectives Brush Creek and the surrounding towns has ever had. She's given up on the idea of marriage—and pleasing her mother—and has dedicated herself fully to her job. Which is great, since one of the most perplexing cases of her career has come to town. Kyler Fuller thinks he's finally ready to move past the woman who ghosted him years ago. He's cut his hair, and he's ready to start dating. Too bad every woman he's been out with is about as interesting as a lamppost—until Dahlia. He finds her beautiful, her quick wit a breath of fresh air, and her intelligence sexy. Can Kyler and Dahlia use their faith to find a way through the obstacles threatening to keep them apart?

A Partner for the Paramedic: A Fuller Family Novel - Brush Creek Brides Romance (Book 11): Jazzy Fuller has always been overshadowed by her prettier, more popular twin, Fabiana. Fabi meets paramedic Max Robinson at the park and sets a date with him only to come down with the flu. So she convinces Jazzy to cut her hair and take her place on the date. And the spark between Jazzy and Max is hot and instant...if only he knew she wasn't her sister, Fabi.

Max drives the ambulance for the town of Brush Creek with is partner Ed Moon, and neither of them have been all that lucky in love. Until Max suggests to who he thinks is Fabi that they should double with Ed and Jazzy. They do, and Fabi is smitten with the steady, strong Ed Moon. As each twin falls further and further in love with their respective paramedic, it becomes obvious they'll need to come clean about the switcheroo sooner rather than later...or risk losing their hearts.

A Catch for the Chief: A Fuller Family Novel - Brush Creek Brides Romance (Book 12): Berlin Fuller has struck out with the dating scene in Brush Creek more times than she cares to admit. When she makes a deal with her friends that they can choose the next man she goes out with, she didn't dream they'd pick surly Cole Fairbanks, the new Chief of Police. Not only is Cole twelve years older than Berlin, he doesn't date. Period.

His friends call him the Beast and challenge him to complete ten dates that summer or give up his bonus check. When Berlin approaches him, stuttering about the deal with her friends and claiming they don't actually have to go out, he's intrigued. As the summer passes, Cole finds himself burning both ends of the candle to keep up with his job and his new relationship. When he unleashes the Beast one time too many, Berlin will have to decide if she can tame him or if she should walk away.

ABOUT LIZ

Liz Isaacson writes inspirational romance, usually set in Texas, or Montana, or anywhere else horses and cowboys exist. She lives in Utah, where she teaches elementary school, taxis her daughter to dance several times a week, and eats a lot of Ferrero Rocher while writing. Find her on her website at lizisaacson.com.

Made in the USA
Middletown, DE
14 April 2019